The Zodiac Proposition

JELANI KING

Published by Franklin Publishers
Printed in the United States of America

For permissions, inquiries, or additional copies, contact:
Franklin Publishers
www.franklinpublishers.com

TABLE OF CONTENTS

— CHAPTER 1 —

"So kids, you gonna tell us where the gold is?" one of the pirates leaned over with a menacing snarl.

"NEVER!" Replied Jaden, laughing, just as he closed his mouth and relaxed his facial muscles, POW! A pirate of slender build slugged his lip open. Jaden pressed into the affected area with his tongue. The man had a long chin and a pointed face. His nose was thin and pointy as well, the length going down the majority of his face. "Ow, that one kind've hurt." Jaden was a tall, unusually lanky fellow. He had a long face with a sharp nose that complemented his prominent cheekbones and bright eyes that compared well with his fiery red hair.

"Shut up!" another one of the pirates said, striking him once more. A heavyset man who looked like he weighed about 300 pounds. "Augh, think I lost a tooth that time." Jaden spat out a mixture of blood and spit. "Yeah, definitely loosened up a bit, to say the least, ay Willie." William glared at Jaden. William was about average height for his age. This made him considerably smaller than other children on the island. He had a broad face, which included a dimpled chin, thick upper lip, and eyes as black as the hair ruffled at the top. "Oh, don't be so mad, Willie, I'll make you a deal. After all this is over, I'll take you out for a cider, just me and you, a darling tavern of your choice, and a cider for my best boy. I'll even pay for it this time. Have 'em splash in a lil rum, I prom-" Suddenly, WHAM! Another strike from the heavy-set man. This time with his foot. Jaden rolled over his own bruised cheek, landing on his side. He struggled to get on his knees due to the ropes that bound his arms and wrists.

"We're not here to play games." The captain announced, a man of average stature, built with muscle and donning a blonde mustache-goatee combo. He pulled his pistol out, and the last remaining bar patrons scurried to get out, panicking like tree rodents after a bolt of lightning had lit their branch aflame. The room was clamoring with screams and breaking glass, along with many other distinguished thuds.

"Now tell me where the gold is, or I'll start shooting." He threatened, aiming the gun at the small gap between the two boys. "First at your kneecaps, then your fingers, and lastly, those clean-shaven, charming faces of yours."

"O sugar, flattery will get you nowhere." Jaden retorted, prompting the heavy-set man to lift his arms to strike him again.

"Okay! Fine, fine." He negotiated in a rushed manner, intent on not being struck, "I'll give you the location of the sapphires."

"Gold."

"The Diamonds."

"Gold."

"The emeralds?"

"Oh-ho-ho, you must think you're the cock of the walk?" The robust pirate raised his gun, "Don't think I won't pull the trigger? I'm Samuel Cheers, the baddest pirate to land on this isle. I put holes through three people in this here village this morning alone! Now you better tell me where the gold is, son!"

"Fine," Jaden said, his tone completely serious now. "To get to the gold, you have to blow on a magic flute."

"Magic flute?"

"Yeah, and lucky for you, I happen to own the only magic flute on the island." Jaden smiled as his tooth plopped to the ground.

"Well, hot damn, I knew you'd come around, lil' buddy. Where's this magical flute-a-majig? Just let me blow it, and I'll be getting ye and yer lil buddy on your way to church or schooling or whatever the hell kids do on this daggummit island."

"Okay, the location of the magic flute is…"

"Yeah?"

"Let me finish."

"The magic flute's location is…"

"Well, spit it out already boy!"

"In my pants."

"What? You mean like in your pocket?"

"No, in my pants."

"What?"

"The magical flute is in my pants."

"Huh?"

"It's my dick."

"What?"

"The magical flute is my penis."

"GODDAMMIT! I've wasted enough time on you Junior; maybe a limp will make you a lil' less hard-headed."

"Awww man," Jaden said, laughing. He closed his eyes, bowed his head, and waited until he heard a bang. He looked up and, to his surprise, saw Samuel's chest covered in blood, the balls of lead protruding from the tears in his blouse. The captain's eyes rolled into the back of his head, and he fell back-first onto the cold, hardwood-paneled ground with a dubious thud. The other pirates were all silent in their confusion as they watched their dead captain lying on the ground. They stared back at where the bullet came from, the middle-aged bartender, Walter. Standing upright, holding a double-barrelled carbine rifle, still aiming where Samuel Cheers once stood. An eye still shut.

"Now the rest of y'all better scram ya hear me? Even though there's eight of ya, I still got a couple left in the chamber and a whole lotta fight left in my heart." Walter was a tall, burly old man; he had a deep, powerful voice that shook mountains when he spoke and sharp eyes that cut deep into even the bravest man's soul. A square face, mahogany skin, and a tuft of greying black hair swirling atop his head. "I'm serious, scram." He said as he fired randomly into the crowd. It was enough to get the pirates going, at least. They all charged the door at once, some tripping out, others being pushed, but in a matter of seconds, the tavern was cleared.

"You boys okay?" Walter asked whilst walking around the bar table, carefully examining for any leftover pirates.

"Yeah, we're good," William responded. Walter began untying them.

"Thanks, Walter man, I'm not sure what we would do if you weren't on duty tonight," Jaden said, relieved.

"We could've just told them we didn't know where the friggin gold was in the first place."

"But then William, my boy, they would've killed us," Jaden said, freeing himself of the last coil of rope.

"Not if you never said 'ooo me! Me! I know where the gold is, but a girl's gotta have her secrets, or is it a magician never reveals their tricks?' Yeah, that one. I think that was the bullshit you pulled this time."

"Oh yeah," Jaden replied, his twisted sense of humor having seemed to return, "and then I got punched onto the table." He smiled, reaching for the affected area of his jaw as he sighed deeply. "Good times."

"Yeah, I'm just glad they were too busy pummeling you to get in any good hits on me," William proceeded to stand up.

"Are you jealous?"

"No."

"I'm sorry, did you want bruises the size of peaches on your back?"

"It's not like that at all. I'm not jealous."

"This one's swelling like a nectarine. You want a tangerine to match up."

"Jaden-"

"Wanna go find the pirates so you can also get painted black and blue, sweety?" Jaden said mockingly.

"I'm not jealous," William muttered under his breath. "I'm tired, Jaden. We keep doing the same shit day after day. Fighting pirates was cool when we were younger, but I don't know man, it feels like we're not even making a difference."

"The whole kill all pirates' revenge schtick getting old? Yeah, I can feel that in my back."

"Seriously, Jaden, you don't ever wonder if there's more than this island?"

"I've got my best friend, good food, and adventure. Sure, there's more, but who needs it?" Jaden smiled at William, and William returned the look with a heavy resignation hanging over his eyelids. Walter was brandishing glasses with spit and an old cloth that may have been clean several years ago, but now was almost as black as charcoal. He listened intently to their conversation. He had been using the same motion for a couple minutes in the same spot on the glass, drawn into his own epiphany.

"It just feels like a rut, dude. No matter how many pirates we kill, they keep coming." William hung his apron on the seat of the stool, near one of the legs. He could see a brownish stain at the edge of the fold. He picked up the apron and let it spread from the collar of his white button-up shirt nearly to the ground, examining the various dirt and blood stains. It wasn't his blood, and he hadn't made the mess, but it still fell on him to manage.

"Hence the *kill all pirates* revenge schtick." Jaden pulled a stool beside his friend.

"Chill out. It's not a schtick, and it's not revenge." William balled up the apron and used it as a seat cushion.

"No, I know you're honoring the victims or taking responsibility. But dude, I was one of those victims, and I do feel a bit honored."

One cider." William said to Walter, who paid no attention.

"Cider? Why the hell are you getting a cider at this hour, dude?"

"I don't know man, I feel like cider can't really explain it."

"Very weird feeling, but all right, spend it if you got it."

"Yeah, plus, you know, you're paying for it and all."

"Paying? Says who?"

"Says you! Remember, it was like five minutes ago. You promised me if we got out of this, you'd buy me a cider."

"I did, didn't I?" Jaden recalled wistfully.

"Yeah man, sure, I'm positive you didn't get hit that hard. Hey Walter, make sure to leave the rind, gives it the kick." William threw in. Walter gave him a resigned, stoic look, finished polishing his glass and sighed deeply. He got to work on the ciders while the two boys finished up their conversation.

"Damn, this sucks. To tell you the truth, I didn't think we were gonna make it out of that one."

"What?"

"We were tied up by bloodthirsty armed scoundrels being beaten mercilessly, I mean, granted, we've got out of a lot of situations, but this time, we may as well have been knocking on heaven's door."

"Wait, you didn't know Walter was here and planned this from the beginning, realizing we'd get out of our predicament unscathed?" William inquired with a diminishing sense of wonder.

"Nah man, I was just being a wise ass." Jaden cackled.

"I'm going to kill you."

"What?" Jaden laughed heavier.

"You were planning to let me get shot in the face in the name of *adventure*!" William slowly realized his pal's intention.

"Hey," Jaden's tone calmed. "Don't forget the kneecaps."

William pounced on Jaden, throwing both of their bodies to the floor and began to ring his neck.

"I'm gonna kill you!" William shouted. All the while, Jaden laughed. The boys tousled and turned on the floor when suddenly they were interrupted by the clanging of glass on the table. They both looked over to see three very delectable ciders foaming on the countertop.

"Hey Walter, I'm only paying for one drink. You do know that, right?" Jaden said to the worn tavern owner. Walter, who was already turned around, polishing his wares, just waved a hand.

"Cool. Thanks, Mr. Barkeep," Jaden said.

"Yeah, thanks, Walter," William chimed in.

Walter turned around and placed his hands firmly on the counter.

"You too, missy. I know you don't think I'm the one who's going to be drinking this garbage." Jaden and William turned around, puzzled to see a little brunette girl with an unkempt light-brown ponytail squirm from underneath one of the tables. She had a small, mousy face, bright hazel eyes, cupid-bow lips and a round forehead.

"Thanks, Walter, I really didn't think you saw me that time," she said bashfully, fixing her hair.

"Laila! My childhood friend!" Jaden exclaimed, slapping his knee. "I should've seen that coming. Why are you here?"

"We're not friends. I was down by the old school when I saw Sydney chasing away some pirates. I kept close to them just in case they were up to something. Saw you get punched and thought you were really going to die," she chuckled. "I didn't wanna miss that."

"What?" Jaden gasped. "Then why didn't you just reveal yourself after the pirates left?"

"I figured William would kill you, and that might not have happened if I were there."

"Oh, it definitely would have," William responded casually.

"And when that failed?"

"I figured Walter would do the trick." Laila shrugged. They both peered over the bar to see Walter brandishing his shotgun. He looked at them somberly until they turned around.

"Yeah, that is a probable cause now that I think about it," Jaden went back to sipping his cider. Laila joined in and sat on the barstool.

"Here, I figured you'd need this," Laila brought out a damp cloth and unraveled it to reveal a glass cup. Unbeknownst to William, she had run the cup under cool water. William reached for the cup before Laila pulled it back. "Let me. I've learned that cold helps with swelling." Laila lifted William's shirt and pressed the cool cloth on the skin of his back. His body tensed on contact but relaxed shortly afterward.

"Where'd you learn that?" Jaden asked, leaning over the counter. She stirred the drink a bit before taking a sip.

"William." Laila looked up from her glass mid-drink. Her eyes widened, and she began to chug the beverage before slamming it down and returning both of her hands to William's back.

"Wow, Walter, this is a good cider. You've outdone yourself!" Laila appraised the bartender's skill, and Walter once more raised his hands and got back to polishing his wares.

"Ciders are amazing, but do you remember that milk cake from the bandit's birthday party?" Jaden slammed the drink down on the table like an old drunkard.

"God, Jaden! Relax! It wasn't- wait, was I even there yet?" Laila questioned before sipping her drink.

"Not from what I remember." William raised his eyebrows and leaned further on the bar.

The three kids talked about their adventures, joking about old times. One of those good-natured conversations where one laughs over their own words before speaking. This continued long after they had finished their drinks.

"It's time for you kids to leave," Walter said.

"Yeah, it is getting kind've late, isn't-" William's thought was made clearer by his yawn. Jaden popped out of his chair over to the broken wooden table. He picked up a scarf and tossed it over his neck.

"Alright, I've got all my things. C'mon, Laila, I'll take you home today."

"No, I want William to do it."

"O, so now you and William are a thing? What happened to not wanting to ruin friendships?"

"I just like that he actually walks me home instead of walking me to his house, telling me this is my home now and leaving when I won't go inside."

"Home is where the heart is, and I feel so at home with you." Jaden interlaced his fingers, making a kissy face in her direction.

"Okay, that's it, time to leave," Walter added

"Alright," Jaden saluted the old bartender. "Same time tomorrow, Walter?"

"No, I don't think you understand, not go. I want you boys to leave and never come back here." Walter replied.

"What? Why?" William asked.

"You kids are banned from my bar. You are not allowed to come back here ever again." Walter looked between the two with the same sharp eyes he narrowed before firing at the pirates.

"Walter, I live here, and I work here... You can't really afford to lose staff."

"I'll tell you what I can't afford, William. A broken table, bullet holes in my walls, and not to mention a big, dead pirate corpse lying in the middle of my floor!

"Yeah, you should really get rid of that. It's kinda starting to stink." Jaden added.

"Jaden, not helping!" Laila exclaimed.

"It all needs to stop now. I gave you boys plenty of chances, figured as you got older, maybe you'd mature, but I've had it. You two need to get out of my bar and never come back." Walter announced as he dropped the carbine rifle on the table.

"Walter, we'll pay for it, it's alright."

"Okay, William, let's pretend for a second that you actually could pay for the damages, " Walter poured a bluish liquid on the rag that half-explained the darkened color. "That you had an actual income that I don't supply and are financially stable." He squeezed the rag and twisted it with his oak-branch-like fingers. "There'd still be a big- now, may I add, a smelly pirate corpse in the middle of my bar, and shootouts aren't as good for business as you'd think." Walter had squeezed most of the moisture by one-handing the cloth.

"This is really kind, 've a dig at the employer- and that's you." Jaden chimed in.

"Since when have you cared about business?" Laila asked, dumbfounded.

"William, you're fired. You three need to get out of my bar now." Walter threw down the rag, and it was so dry it fell onto the countertop without so much as a plop.

"I mean, some new rags would really drive up business," Jaden added.

"What are kids doing hanging out in a bar anyways? Doesn't this island have a church? Or garden? Or field? Some large recreational area you all can play in?" Walter asked, becoming more uncertain of the answer. An uncertainty that was quickly picked up and preyed upon.

"But Walter, I didn't do anything," Laila said, innocently twisting a foot in the ground and looking up from a lowered gaze. Her doe-eyed expression made it impossible for any adult to resist her cuteness. She had swindled many out of candy, money, and even meals on occasion.

"I know," Walter sighed deeply. "But there really shouldn't be kids in this bar, which is why in a few years, when you're 16, you can come back here. Jaden and William, you two are banned for life." Walter pointed at the two of them, resting one hand on the countertop.

"Ah, man," William pleaded. "Walter, man, don't do this to me."

"Suck it up Willie," Jaden added callously, his face turned to the ground.

"It's obvious we're not wanted here. If it's one thing Walter taught us, it's to not stay where we're not wanted, right? We entered this bar as boys. We should at least leave like men." A single teardrop fell to the floor from his eyes and made a deafening pop as it hit the hardwood panel. Jaden was rather tall for his age, but ever since he was twelve, he had a fortunate growth spurt and grew to be quite tall. There wasn't much development on his muscles at his age, and it left his limbs looking rather gangly. Still, he was tall enough to almost look Walter in the eye as he sniffled and broke composure. "Is that man enough for you, Walter?" Jaden said through sobs, "Look, I could be growed up. Please don't make us leaveee, Walter; we have nowhere else to go!" Jaden bawled.

"That's it, I've had enough!" Walter exclaimed. He picked up the shotgun and cocked it with one hand. If this bar isn't cleared in 5 seconds, there's gonna be a few new additions to the scenery and a lot more decomposing messes to clean up."

"Please, Walter, I don't have anyone else." William pleaded

"5!" That was all it took. The kids took flight out of the bar, jumping over broken tables and Cheers to leave as fast as possible. They were all outside the tavern and took one last look before continuing onwards through the town. It was an unusually starry night, each rock along the path shorn with an unmistakable luster keen of magic and whimsy.

"I can't believe Walter really did that," William said. "I know it was just a job, but I thought-."

"I was pretty sure he was my dad," Jaden added. Both William and Laila looked at him, puzzled.

"You live with your dad," William said.

"Yeah, but he's never home," Jaden responded.

"Your dad's white."

"Don't be racist, William."

"It's not about the damage. We know that much. " Laila said monotonously.

"Walter doesn't raise an eyebrow when he's upset, much less his voice. Even when I gave him the look, he didn't react. It was like he looked past me. I know that face. He's possessed."

They instantly directed their attention towards her lament. "It's the only explanation nobody can resist my teary-eyed stares unless they've had direct contact with the dark forces. And those were real tears." She turned her gaze away from the ground and faced the two boys with the same teary-eyed stare she held earlier. "Yep, darkness.." The emotion disappeared from her face entirely, and she returned to staring at the ground with the same inquisitive look.

"Ever think maybe you're losing your touch?" Jaden responded slyly. "Losing a lil bit of this," he pinched her cheek and held the skin tightly, much to her aggravation. "Gaining a lot more of this," he reached for her rear end, but Laila grabbed his arm in time. She smacked him, leaving a red imprint on his cheek that he laughed off and seemed unfazed by. He looked into her eyes, tears rolling down his face. "WHY YOU GOTTA BE LIKE THAT LAILA!" He began bawling his eyes out and proceeded to run ahead of the pair.

"I think what Jaden was trying to say is maybe your endearing charm is being replaced by a more alluring- comeliness."

"What the fuck are you saying?" Laila asked crudely.

"I'm just saying that Walter and other men may stop categorizing you as daddy's little girl."

"And start wanting to play house." Jaden interrupted, popping out from behind the pair.

Laila's face turned a deep, shaded red. The comment seemed to stop her in her tracks completely. She had her hands behind her back, looked to the ground and started twisting her foot in the dirt like an adolescent schoolgirl.

"And what do you wanna play, William?" she tugged his shirt, looking up at him, arching her eyebrows.

"Not this," he said casually, continuing his walk.

"Awwww. You're no fun anymore," she sighed. "You know the old William would have gone catatonic." They continued walking and laughing, enjoying their night, forgetting all their worries. Eventually, they reached the coastline, and it was beautiful, woven with stars that shone brightly. Illuminating the water so that even the fish and seaweed were visible. There was a small boat docked by a bridge. The boat wasn't as grandiose as the schooners that coasted by or the galleons that docked on either side of the island. It was a modest ship, with one mast and barely any legroom due to the various packages and supplies crowding the deck. There were patches on the hull where it looked like the boat had hit a sharp rock or a hard wave. The boat wasn't much, but the wind whispered into the anchored sails a note louder than any pirate they left behind. Freedom. Jaden lay in the cool, soft sand, pulling William's leg, who turned his attention from the boat and laid by his side. Laila sat holding her knees. They all looked up at the sky, enamored by its full beauty and for just a while, forgot all their troubles, gazing upon the celestial magnificence. "It really is a beautiful night tonight, isn't it?" Laila stared up into the spangled horizon.

"Yeah, but you would probably be able to see how truly awesome it is if you just lay down," Jaden winked, patting the spot beside the scarf tail.

"I don't want to lay down anywhere near you," she responded cholerically.

"No, seriously, it's incredibly beautiful from this angle."

"Yeah, but I have hair. I don't want to get it all sandy."

"It's worth it, trust me." He pulled her by the back of her shirt. She held the tail end down with both hands, keeping the shirt in place. No support to hold her upright. Her head slammed into the sand, and she just lay there. Arms still covering her chest, knees bent, surveying the beautiful night sky.

"Yeah, this may be worth it," she muttered timidly.

They stared in silence, watching the sky, wishing and hoping every night could be like this. Shining with an otherworldly luster, nothing but dreams and magic flying through the atmosphere. The kids closed their eyes and took it all in. Tonight, all their worries would be enveloped by the night sky, and the shine of their ambition would become visible at daybreak.

William awoke on the sand next to his friend Jaden. He stretched with a yawn and shook the grains from his hair. He tapped his sleeping friend to wake him up, but he did not budge a muscle. William got up and walked towards the water. He knelt down by the ocean and started rinsing his face with the sea. He stared at his reflection for a while and then looked once more at the horizon. It was beautiful. The sun was coming up, and the sea sparkled with a luster reminiscent of the stars. William removed his shoes, rolled his pant legs and soaked them in the cool water. He kicked his feet around, splashed in the cool, clear liquid and hung his head back. He knew that he would need to wake his friend soon before the sun came out and burned their skin, but for now, he was enjoying the peace and serenity.

"Well, well, what do we have here?" said a gruff voice from afar. William turned around to see remnants of misfits from the other day. One of the vagabonds, a stocky, fat pirate, walked over to his friend. He kicked Jaden in the ribs, a fairly soft kick compared to the damage he seemed capable of, but the boy didn't budge. The pirate unholstered his gun and pointed it directly towards Jaden's temple. William sighed deeply, covered his ears and continued to kick his feet.

The pirate lowered the gun and placed it next to the sleeping boy's ear. Now aimed away from his face entirely. He pulled the trigger, and a loud bang echoed all across the beach, scattering the seagulls into the salty air.

"Why won't you wake up!" The gun-toting pirate hollered. He picked Jaden up, "Wake up!" He smacked Jaden square in the cheek. "Wake up!" He smacked him again. He kept this up for a while until he finally decided to throw Jaden, who simply tumbled across the sand in ragdoll fashion, not separating one eyelid. "This kid is more trouble than he's worth. As acting captain, I say we put a bullet in his face and let him get all the rest he deserves. All in favor, say aye!"

"Aye!" They all yelled except for the acting captain.

"Good," he said. He held up his gun, put it directly on Jaden's temple and shot a lead bullet directly into Jaden. His eyes lit up as he gasped his last breath. They rolled back into his head as he grasped for air and dear life. The haunting sound of his breath being cut short made a few of them cringe, and the boy with fiery hair lay pale, lifeless and covered with sand. William sighed once more and continued kicking his feet. The pirates all cheered.

"Aye, the red menace is no more." They danced and sang a jaunty tune about the Cheers pirates.

"Meat, mead, and vengeance back at Walter's, then we can leave this accursed land and finally put our captain's spirit to rest." The stout, violent man who was now acting captain directed. Suddenly, they all heard a splash. They turned around at once to see if it was a spectator who had witnessed their heinous deeds; they turned to see William kicking his feet as if nothing unusual had occurred.

"Well, well, well, we meet again," the stout man declared with a sweet, prideful intonation.

"You ready to suffer the same fate as your friend there?" He pointed the gun towards William, and just then, Jaden came out of the water naked as the day he'd been born.

"What's all this commotion that I can hear from the ocean?" he said with a scowl, acting as if nothing was out of the ordinary. He knocked some water out of his ear.

"You!" The pirate shouted. "But I just put a bullet in you!"

"Really now? A bullet? Cause this body seems relatively non-penetrated from my point of view, but that depends where you poi-" he was cut off by the firing of a round drilling deep into his skull. This time, he fell back into the ocean without so much as a whimper. Strangely enough, not even a splash. The pirate turned around.

"I could swear I killed the brat last time."

All that was behind him was a ruffled old T-shirt and a pair of shorts. The pirate turned back, and directly in his view was Jaden grinning wildly. He tried to jump back, but just then, Jaden embraced him tightly and pressed a cold glass shard against the man's neck.

"Men! Men!" He screamed. "Don't just stand there. Do something,"

"I think they should sit back," Jaden said, sliding the shard across his neck, drawing blood.

"David!" one of the men shouted.

"What do you want!" Another screamed.

"Good point." Jaden chuckled in his air of indifference. "I don't want anything from you filthy bilge rats." He gripped David's head tightly, still holding the shard that was now glowing to an almost neon as the sun hit the glass.

"You monster!" A pirate shouted. He reached for his own gun and then aimed it at Jaden, who ducked behind David.

"Now find your ship or find your grav- Oh shit," Jaden had stumbled, not only with his wording but combined with the weight of his captive and the shifting material where he found footing, the shard had been fatally driven into David's neck. The eruption of a major artery painted Jaden's dumbfounded expression. Jaden dropped the body to the ground and raised his hands, but the pirates had taken heed of his prior message. The pirates tripped over themselves once more, leaving their weapons and their acting captain, who writhed around in pain, trying to cover the gash in his neck. Jaden yawned, walked over to the pile of clothes and collected them. He put on his pants and shirt, when suddenly his eyes widened. "Oh no, where is it, where is it?" he looked left to right frantically, dropped to the ground and started digging wildly. "Oh no. Oh no," piles of sand built up around him. "Yes!" Jaden exclaimed. "I found you," he picked up a dusty, old trinket, a plain black string bracelet with about two or three charms on it.

"3," Jaden said, breaking the fourth wall. He was right, but none of those charms count Jaden. He walked towards the clear, crystal ocean, over to where William sat and began washing his face.

"My god, the blood's getting off of my skin but not my clothes."

"Why would you put them on before washing it off?" William entertained.

"I figured it wouldn't set in so quickly."

"It's blood. Why take the risk? Now you've gotta stroll the town looking like you were rolling around in Sam's butcher shop."

"Dude, it's red... The water's blue, so I assumed I'd just have purple on me. Who knew it'd still be red? You really do learn something new every day."

"William!" A voice called from the distance. The boys paused their argument for a brief moment and looked back. It was Laila, wading through the sand.

"William! Other one!" she called again.

"Over here!" Jaden shouted. Laila ran over there as fast as her little legs could carry her. She looked the two boys up and down.

"Blood-stained shirt? Ruffled shorts? Corpses? Did Jaden die?!" She gasped and shook her tiny fists excitedly.

"Hey, are you using that shirt by any chance?" Jaden asked, his swimmer's body outline slightly inflating his six-pack.

Laila looked down at the clothes in her hand.

"These are for William," she responded with gritted teeth, trying to uphold her cheery temperament.

"I get it, appreciate the view."

Laila shrugged off the comment and continued walking towards the water, where William sat, still calmly kicking his feet.

"I brought you some of my dad's old clothes," she stated demurely.

"Your dad's a pretty huge guy. I doubt that I could fit anything he wore."

"That's why I said old. They should be just about your size by now."

"Thanks, but no thanks." William sighed deeply. "I'm not the one drenched in another man's fluids." They turned to see Jaden in his bloodstained clothes, burying the captain in the sand, patting the breast-shaped mounds he created.

"Ooo, captain, you're so voluptuous," he said in a deep, not really seductive tone. She turned to William. "Not until he washes the rest off." They turned back to see Jaden rubbing his face all over the disintegrating breast-shaped mounds.

"I hate him." Laila snarled.

"Jaden!" William yelled.

— CHAPTER 2 —

"I still don't see why we had to throw my old clothes into the ocean," Jaden whined.

"Water is clear, Jaden, not blue," William replied, annoyed.

"Blue or clear, that was my favorite blouse." They ignored his comment.

"Thanks, Laila, this shirt is extra comfy. Is this cotton?"

"Sheep wool." Laila brushed a light white thread from the hem of her skirt, and, in the same motion, reached for one of her light-brown hairs, twisting it as if she brushed a loose strand from the garment.

"Ooo, even better," he said excitedly. "It's so comfy and warm and a little bit too warm, actually," Jaden pulled the collar of the shirt a bit too hard, and they heard the small snapping of fabric. Almost instantly, he felt a red stinging across his face and looked up to a frustrated Laila, one hand still raised, brow furrowed, eyes nearly in tears.

"Don't stretch it!" she said with the most disdainful bass her shrill voice could muster.

"Did you just smack me?" Jaden asked dubiously. Laila stood with her fists balled to her side, shaking with contempt.

"Laila, whoa, calm down. It's just one of your dad's old shirts," William added.

"I mean, it didn't hurt. It was just really fast." Jaden continued. Laila folded her arms, pouted and walked ahead at a quicker pace.

"Good for you," Jaden joined in her stride. "Look, I'm sorry for stretching your dad's shirt, Laila."

"Please just shut up."

"I truly do apologize to you and your dad."

"Go away."

"Truly, I mean it. Especially if it was his favorite."

"Where are we even walking to?" William pondered as they continued blindly down their path.

The kids stopped and saw that inches away from them stood the back of an old moss-covered wall. The plaster was peeling, and the paint had different hues of white in certain areas.

"This is-" William's voice broke, and his head briefly dropped before he pulled it back up and looked towards the group, whose gloomy expressions still focused on the tangles of moss covering the peeling tavern wall. Moss that either fixed the chips to the wall, prevented them from falling, or grew over the patches entirely.

"It's just a force of habit. I didn't mean," Laila's eyes shifted and her brow furrowed as her arms crossed.

"It's okay. Walter's place is at least closer to town. Definitely a lot closer than my place." William replied, his words trailing off as he turned away from the old tavern.

"Do you need a minute to go inside?" Laila offered a little more than suggestion.

"Let's just keep walking." William brushed aside the comment.

They walked for miles in complete and total silence. Even Jaden was speechless. He opened his mouth on multiple occasions, making it seem as if he had something to say but could never find the right words. Laila just walked, head held in the direction she was going, posture perfectly upright. William had his hands in his pockets, looking towards the ground, kicking a couple of rocks as he passed. They came to a very eerie-looking area where the trees were skinny at the bottom, but the leaves on top were bunched up enough to give it a permanent sense of night, if any time of day entered. The only light was the one that shone from where they were standing. Further in, it seemed to become pitch black.

"The Black Wood," William said, his voice once again losing air and resonance. The wind chilled him deeper than any cold.

"Where it all began," Jaden continued. The branches of the trees swayed like they were trying themselves to avoid the cool wind, and whispered as the breeze whistled around the gaps where they failed to divert the frigid air, which scattered leaves throughout the forest, despite not even a fleck of pollen finding itself out of the perpetual night-time shade of the trees.

"Guys, can we please get out of here? This place gives me the creeps. Let's go, let's go," Laila said, pulling on the two. The pair inched away, still in awe of the woods. Laila tugged their sleeves with her eyes shut tight. The sound of a woman's cackle rings out, but it seems only Jaden and William can hear it. They shudder and begin walking away from the eerie woods.

"To think that all happened only three years ago." William started.

"Three years can be a long time on this island," Laila said.

"Not long enough," he shook his head to intercept his flashback.

"Even if hundreds of years pass, it will never be long enough, William," she fumed, growing weary of William's guilt.

"Truer words have never been spoken." He felt his chest as if a sharp pain had gone through the area.

"You did what you thought was best. Nobody could have known." Jaden put a hand on William's shoulder.

"The adults knew... My parents knew."

"You help people, William. It's just who you are." Laila avoided his gaze. She refused to give too much attention to anything that could change the way she saw him, even if that meant averting her gaze from what was directly in front of her eyes.

"It's who I was," William stated resolutely. He clenched his fist to the point his arm shook with a small tremor. Silence swallowed the group once more. They all became flustered by their inability to respond rather than the knowledge of what to say. There were enough conversations that ended in shutting down quietly, holing up in a room for several days, or the risk-taking behavior bordering on ideation. It's difficult enough to argue with grief, but when dressed as certainty, the dangers easily outweigh the benefits. They all kept quiet until they came to another coastline.

"It'll be nightfall soon, you know? Wanna camp out here like yesterday?" Jaden yawned and scratched his back.

"No, it's best we get off this side of the island. Who knows what happens there at night?" Laila looked at the boys wide-eyed. Her hand stretched over her mouth with huge remorse for her words. "I'm so sorry. I just meant-"

The worry that filled Jaden's face as his breathing shifted and William's small wince when he reached for his chest showed they knew all too well what happens in the black wood.

"Well, you guys can go if you want. I think this is my bed for the night." Jaden plopped himself in the sand.

"No! No! No! Laila screeched. "Get up! Get up!" She fell to the floor and started hitting him. "

It's just sand, dude, I'll even wash it. Your dad will never notice." William's reply entirely dismissed Laila's intensity. The hits slowed, and she curled in on herself, her balled fists shaking at her side.

"No! No! He's ruining it! He's ruining it!" She closed her eyes, shaking slightly like a cold shiver had run through her spine and the hits were slowed to a complete stop. She buried her face in her arms and lay there.

"Jaden, man, just give her back the shirt. Her dad probably needs it for work or something. You know Laila doesn't lose her cool like that."

"Idiot," Jaden muttered under his breath

"What'd you just call me?" William raised

"Idiot, dummy, jackass, but you probably heard idiot." Jaden smiled.

"Laila, I'll take responsibility for the shirt 'cause this one's about to get covered in blood real soon." William cocked back his fist.

"No!" Laila sprang up and grabbed him. She rubbed a soothing hand down the length of his shoulder before she decked him in the upper arm.

"Ow, the fuck?" William rubbed the area.

"And you still haven't realized?" Jaden hopped up from the sand, using nothing but his arms to propel himself to his legs.

"Realized what?"

"The shirt! It's not her dad's; she made it herself! Idiot!" Jaden pulled Laila out by the hand, "See right there on the tip of her index finger, that little line. It's from a sewing needle." Laila snatched it away from his grasp. She stared down Jaden with an intensity that would make any person at least tense up with the still, controlled breathing of a cat, a few moments before the pounce. "She cut herself making it for you, which is kind've sad, seeing as it looks like she barely got it made. Come on William, you could tell this didn't come from any tailor. The stitch work is so sloppy, and look at this crooked cross-hitch." Jaden laughed, "Doctors; they can reattach fingers to a hand, but let them run into a damn shirt-" Laila struck him across the cheek, leaving another red imprint slightly higher than the last.

"I hate him," she whispered, and was gone.

"Laila!" William turned around to run after her.

"Don't forget this," Jaden said. He threw the dusty shirt from the sand where he lay.

"Jaden, you have to go home eventually, you know."

"Home is where the heart is," Jaden replied, lying bareback on the ground.

William clenched his chest and then ran off behind Laila.

— CHAPTER 3 —

"Laila! Laila!" William called into the night, now wearing the soft wool sweater the girl knitted for him. It was all for naught as he could not catch sight of the girl. It was foggy around this part of the island, and his sight wasn't usually exceptional under normal conditions. "Laila! Laila!" He called as the night enveloped him. "Laila!" He called one last time, desperately. The girl was nowhere to be found. Perhaps she had escaped and was well on her way home. The fog was now thickening at any point other than the forest, which had a misty yet clear view. The night sky provided little illumination anywhere else, and the trees shone with an otherworldly glow. William turned away from the forest, but a gust of wind seemed to blow him in that direction. "Dammit!" William protested. "I'm not going to the forest, so just show me the way out of here." The fog overtook him, but he remained perfectly still. He truly had no desire to go into the forest. He wanted to go back to the sand. He wanted to make more memories of his friends being upset with each other, crying about clothes and fighting over misunderstandings. He had no intention of returning to the world the fog portended. The problems on this side of the fog all seemed so much more manageable. "I'm not going to the forest," Wiliam stated plainly, and sat as the mist crept slowly into his peripheral vision. "I'll just sit right here and-" William turned his head away, but the mist was directly in front. He shot up and realized he was now surrounded by the darkness of the black wood. The cold air tingling his skin, sending a shiver down his neck. "Shit," William uttered, and despite any direction he moved towards, he found himself further away from the light of the clearing.

The next morning, Jaden awoke and stretched in the sand.

"Eesh," he said, kicking off the excess sediment that had accumulated around him. "Must've been a windy night," he said to himself. He sprawled out on the ground, stretching and yawning, before finally getting up and dusting himself off. He stripped his shorts and shook them out. He put them back on and began walking towards the road. He passed the forest and most of the town in his groggy state, ignoring mostly everyone and everything. He picked up a mango off a fruit stand and continued walking. He knew no man would dare say a word to his face. All they'd do is whisper to one another.

"Look, there's the boy they call the Red Menace. I once seen a cannonball hit that boy directly, and the next day, he was just out and about, not a scratch." Jaden continued his walk, taking one bite of the mango before tossing it aside. "I wasn't really hungry anyway," he thought to himself. Jaden walked along the path towards the town square. The butcher closed his window, peering out, crouched under the windowsill. Jaden continued walking a little past the florist, who glared at him, while she clutched a bouquet away from his gaze. The local vagabonds Jean, Dencois and Crishen shook their heads, looking towards the ground. Jaden searched the town square for his friends, but not being able to find Laila nor William, he left before the stares intensified into more gossip. Jaden went trotting down the path leading to his not-so-old schoolyard. He hadn't attended class in almost a year, so he tiptoed to peer inside and check if things were the same since he left. Nothing had changed. The seats were the same, there were the same lame posters hung all around the room, and the abacus still missed a few beads from the time Chesney Adams backed into the teacher's desk. Although there were a few unfamiliar faces, Jaden couldn't tell if those were just kids he didn't recognize before or actual new additions. He searched around the class with his eyes, making faces at his more unfriendly former classmates and looking for some sign, some recognition that he was gone. He couldn't find one. It was like he had faded from the school's memory. He grew restless playing the difference and remembered that Laila still attended regularly. He went from window to window searching for her. Hoping to find her mindlessly staring at the board, pretending she understood everything the teacher said. He shifted back to his former class and watched, tiptoeing from the window. The teacher droned on, and the students sat upright and attentive. He watched them all pretending to listen, sneaking snacks from their desk, trying to care as they waited for it all to be over. He watched the ones who were in their own world. The kids who were nodding off, trying to follow along, and the naturals who sat attentively and took notes. They all wanted to be somewhere else, but were tethered to this routine. Jaden laughed to himself, feeling victorious. He slept when he wanted, ate when he felt the need, and did what he pleased. He crouched lower, pressing his hands against the glass. Somehow, watching the crowded personality of the classroom from outside the window, he felt less alive. No, it made him feel forgotten. It brought him back to that cold, dark place where that hand of ghastly dark tendrils pushed him up into an erratic breathing of cold sweat. Suddenly, he felt a hand touching his back.

"Eep!" he yelled, turning around swiftly and hitting his head on the window. "Ow,"

"Shhhhh," Laila replied. "What are you doing here?"

"A guy can't come visit his best bud at school?"

"Why do you think we're friends? Don't answer that. Where's William? Doesn't he usually keep you company?"

"I can't find him."

"What do you mean you can't find him?" Laila's voice sharpened. Jaden's breath stopped as he hesitated to answer.

"I mean, I searched pretty much everywhere."

"Pretty much everywhere for you, including how many naps?"

"Laila, I've been up all morning looking around town. At this point, the only place he could be is-" Jaden said, his words trailing off. His eyes grew dark, and his usual cheeriness dissolved as the ground took his focus.

"Oh," she replied meekly. The silence became louder than the wind, and she closed her eyes, taking a deep inhale.

"Well then, let's go," she swallowed her anxiety.

"There?!" Jaden's whisper voice peaked to a high-pitched whisper yell. "He might turn up. We could just wait a couple of hours. He'll get hungry and-"

"I think we both know it'll be a while til we see him again if he's with *her*." Laila dusted herself off and bounded off towards the town with Jaden close by.

It was an entirely different walk for Laila. Dolores, the florist, held a bouquet of radiance akin to her own, although the price tag faced the public. Sam, the butcher, opened a window and suddenly started singing over a plate of cured meats. Even the local vagabonds tipped their hats in respect, knowing full well that they could fleece any onlooker too awestruck. They roamed over the hill and downwards through corners and alleyways, but finally, they were there. The clearing at the outskirts of town. Onwards towards the shoddily made cobblestone path and directly in front of the dead wood.

"There it is... We're here," Jaden said, a footfall away from Laila.

"Yep, here we are," Laila replied, the uneasiness in her voice only made more apparent by its shakiness.

"Look, Laila, you don't need to go. I'll go get him. Just go on home, sit this one out. Please. Trust me." Jaden urged.

"No," was all she said before she darted into the woods.

"Way. Too. Don't." Jaden chased after her, pleading, "It's dangerous, really dangerous. This wood changes people forever. It's like all your nightmares and fears put together- no, the wood is actually worse. There's a reason why not even fire can burn in that place. The winds are always cold, and sometimes the ground itself moves you."

"I can't," her voice barely reached his ears.

"What do you mean- you can't? Why-" he said through heavy breaths.

"I already left him once," she looked back at Jaden, tears forming in her clear hazel eyes. Her brow furrowing with sorrow, and her lip quivering with a slight uncertainty. "I just- I just can't do it again,"

"Laila, don't be dumb. That was different, this is different. We were all lucky that time, but this time, god only knows what's going on."

"Shh, did you hear that?" Laila whipped her head to a bush.

"What, no, what is it?" Jaden replied, looking around wildly.

"The sound of you shutting up," Laila continued her way through the eerie wood, and Jaden ran off after her.

These woods were truly peculiar in that everything about them appeared sinister, down to the dirt path the two were traveling on. Ever so often, when the kids wandered aimlessly, a rock appeared to put them back on the right path. Branches would reach out and lightly poke their necks, crawling across their skin. There was virtually no wildlife nor sky. It would seem as if the wood was completely devoid of life. Suddenly, they came upon it, the big mud-covered shack betwixt two peaks. It would have seemed that the original stone that had been used to build it was now under several coats of grime. The only evidence of the material was at the chimney, which billowed a thin, wispy smoke.

"Is this?" Laila asked.

"Definitely," Jaden confirmed her suspicions. The dirty old house was covered in centuries of filth. Laila inched towards the old, muddy shack and up the old, muddy stairs to the old muddy doorknob that she opened with a piercing creak. She stared into the blackness of the old shack. For a while, it seemed like the only light coming from the house was from the woods. The darkness stretched far into the reaches of the old shack, twisting and jostling menacingly. The light from behind her began fading away into the same twisting darkness. The dark reached out, coiling around her like vines. Lies, insecurities, and other thoughts she pushed away filled her mind, the tendrils pulling and releasing so she spent just enough time in the reality, struggling towards light that her heart sank to the same depth each time the dark appendage filled her mind with misery. She wrestled with it, occasionally going directly through the restraints. Other times, holding on as it spread on contact. The light faded and left nothing to tangibly grasp. She screamed, but it was silent. Reaching back to the light, she fell further into the delusions. There was now only darkness. The whispers, lies, and appendages had vanished, leaving no trace of their existence or the girl, who dared to approach the witch's cottage.

— CHAPTER 4 —

Laila shook and grabbed at the tendrils, tearing darkness from her body until the appendages began to dissipate into the nether.

"So what is this you outgrowing me?"

The words rang through her head as each tendril wormed its way around her skin. She knew they weren't her words, but she could feel everything from the day her bag fell off the wooden stool and the red leather-bound book slipped out onto the floor. These weren't her words, but this was her voice. The thoughts enraged her to the point where she would singularly rip the appendages, only to find a multitude growing in their place.

"It's not fair. Things used to be fair." The voices seemed to come from nowhere and everywhere, as the tendrils had spread further throughout Laila's body. She coughed, half-expecting some water to come out. She had never felt so helpless in that moment, which is why she felt such a burning resentment hearing those same words in her voice.

"You'll know it's real when it can't be outrun." The voice whispered, and the words soothed her for a bit. The words repeated and reverberated through her mind over and over with new contexts of grief. Tears streamed down her cheeks as she pushed through the hall. It took all of her focus to calm, and once her mind was dead silent, a singular thought echoed over its own pronunciation, which made the message difficult to discern.

"That's what you want." The next phrase nearly brought her to her knees and blurred her vision to a point where the tendrils seemed to have doubled. Those words couldn't have been further from the truth, but they pushed more bravery out of her than she'd ever acknowledged. Laila pulled the last of the darkness off her body and spun around, straightening her back. Looking down the winding, twisting hallway, she could hardly see the way back. Having no idea how far the darkness had pulled her in, still, William was nowhere to be seen, so she ascertained it wasn't far enough. Laila made her way through the dark hall for what seemed like hours, enduring the words and reverberations of truths that were left with little examination. She walked until her feet were sore and her toes tingled with blood pooling to the skin, before finally reaching an eerily lit area. She sprinted to the light, turned and burst into the room.

"Eep," she squealed as she waved her arms, trying to regain her balance. She was beginning to take a step back onto the more stable footing towards the door when she heard a couple of voices.

"It's been so long since I've seen you Do you still like carrots I can add some carrots if that's more your appetite" It was a shrill, feminine voice. The voice sounded no older than 19, maybe 20.

"I'd rather not eat anything that goes in this water."

Laila knew that one. It was unmistakable. She could feel her heart shoot through the air, and this may be what prompted her to step off the ledge.

"William!" She squealed as she dove into the big, deep, burnt pot. She jumped on him and held onto the back of his neck. "I missed you," she said, smiling. She held onto his soaking body, too involved in her rhapsody to take note that the boy was shirtless, his hands had been tied behind his back, and all of his scars, including the ominous one that lay across his chest, were visible. She held him as tightly as she could and shut her eyes tighter. Whichever predicament she had saved him from could be explained later. Right now, he was okay, and they had found each other once more. She drew herself back and grinned, looking into his eyes.

"I missed you too," he looked to the side of the pot with a pained, dissatisfied expression. It must have been the lighting, and of course, she knew he didn't have emotions, but he could at least pretend to be happy to see her, after all, she did rescue him; it's not like she was intruding. She felt a frigid poke on her back and turned around. Before her skin could rise, the pale hand smacked her square across the face. She fell into the water and realized it had been much hotter and deeper than she had noticed. She swam around trying to find the surface when she felt a foot mush her head. Another hit, and another as she was being stomped on by her adversary. Laila, losing breath, grabbed the attacker's foot and reached up to the waist, pulling herself up to finally get a good look at the witch. Laila was ashamed to admit it to herself, but the being was truly enchanting. Diamond eyes, starry teeth, and skin glowing with an otherworldly texture were only comparable to that of a goddess. Then the hair, beautiful wavy hair, looked like it could only have been weaved by the fates themselves, each thread glowing with the same ethereal luminescence. Every feature, down to the curve of the ankle, didn't just radiate beauty, but confidence and control. Laila had never felt such admiration for an appearance or been in awe of such a presence. The witch reached out to attack Laila, but despite her speed, she didn't move an inch. Laila welcomed the assault, almost appreciative to be granted the honor of being imprinted on by such beauty. In an instant, William stood between the two, not phased by the blow he had just taken to the chest. He nestled his face in the neck of the witch and entangled their body together. They floated there for a while, intertwined in each other's bodies, spirits resonating, heartbeats synchronizing. Almost one entity, floating in the ever-reaching abyss. Then, the pot collapsed. The side with Laila was the first to go. She had punched the side of the pot in frustration, mistaking the material for something metallic. The cracks appeared first, and as the water pushed its way through, they began to fragment, then the shards dissolved before the pot itself crumbled away into the darkness. The water immediately drenched the coals that were kept ablaze, and Laila fell to one side. The witch fell atop William, and the steam from their encounter beaded the water across their bare bodies. The only luminescence arriving from the sheen in the witch's ethereal locks.

"I'm so sorry that I didn't mean to I mean I don't mind but I didn't mean to"

"Can you get off me?" William said now with a hint of detest in his voice.

"What happened baby You were more than interested before" an icy finger traced a sharp nail across his scar.

William looked back, agitation plain on his face, and the witch hopped off him in an instant. The threads weaved by the fates themselves were banded into a ponytail, and the vivacious figure obscured by crossed arms. "That's all huh" the piercing gaze stared into Laila's eyes so intensely the girl put her head down. "Thought that'd be tougher" the witch said, hips sauntering into the darkness.

William hopped up, made sure his hands were free and shuffled through the darkness til he found her.

"Laila, Laila, Laila," he whispered. He turned around and felt the warm drops go cold on his skin. Even in the darkness and quiet of the room, he could hear her quiet sobs and even see her hazel eyes welling up with despair.

"What? What is she to you?" Laila finally uttered, choking on her words.

William hugged her and pressed her head to his chest. "Nowhere near as important as you." She wanted to pull back but found herself waiting for a pulse and fatigued by that expectation. "You're my light." He whispered into her ear. Laila started sobbing uncontrollably. He wrapped his arm around her tightly and pulled her closer, and closer, and closer. The two holding onto each other as close as two people could in the ever-reaching abyss.

— CHAPTER 5 —

"What the hell was all that about?" Jaden asked wearily.

"We had to talk about some things." William shook off the question.

"Some things like what?"

"I don't know, man… Things."

"Don't give me that, you piece of shit," he grabbed William's collar and mashed it with both thumbs. "You had Laila worried sick!".

"Get off me before I hit you." William shrugged off the grab. "It was a checkup. The witch just had to make sure everything was under control."

"That wasn't a check-up. William, I know those eyes, I know that look better than any-"

"Is it the look of someone who brought tragedy upon his village? Or got his only family killed? Or had his emotions robbed by a witch!" William shot back, and the shock caused Jaden to trip over himself, landing on his backside.

"Sorry man, it just looked like something else, I guess." Jaden stared off to the side, his eyes going dark. He messed his own hair before expressing his usual cheery demeanor.

"What happened?" Jaden asked in a more passive, naive tone.

William had recalled every single moment leading up to the shirt being ripped, from the twisting trails leading him into the woods, to the cobblestone shack with the witch at the door winking at him. He had tried to turn around, but the moment he did, the witch was there, and from the moment he turned back, it was into the dark of the old cobblestone house. A finger was drawn across his chest as a bright glow emanated from the nail, and the shirt was singed apart, glowing a bright-red orange and falling from his shoulders and back. Their lips met with an eruptive passion, and after much unmentionable caressing and fondling, they had gone through the infinite hallway into the giant, burnt pot, where they both fell in with a splash. William threw himself upon the witch, and their lips met once more. His soaking wet pants were now creating a puddle beside the tub, and their bodies intertwined, almost calling to each other simultaneously, before they thrust themselves against each other with such force, they made literal waves.

"I can't seem to recall," William stated.

"Well, you need to apologize to Laila," Jaden said, cooling down.

"Yeah, I was getting to that." William walked over to the girl lying motionless on the sand.

"I'm sorry, Laila. I'll find a way out of this somehow." He said and clenched his teeth

"That's okay, William, I'm just glad you're okay," she replied groggily.

"Okay, up and at 'em," he said, lifting her onto his back.

She instinctively grabbed hold of his neck, and a small grin formed across her face. She buried her face in his scent and fell into a deeper sleep. Her joy still plain as day, widening across her face. He carried her all through town, past the cobblestone path, over the winding hill, through the town square and past the dilapidated burnt houses. The entire area smelled like charcoal and instantaneously brought back the sensation in his nose from the thick smoke of that fateful day. The children pushed on until. Finally, they reached a rather large two-floor estate. The walls of the house were made of stone, but the stone had been painted to resemble the lumber walls used across the town. There was a small veranda that gave the second floor a platform rather than a drop from the window. Inside, the veranda was nearly spotless and almost shone from the moonlight. There was a singular chair rocking in the wind, with a framed portrait of an old woman sitting on the seat. A sign hung on a nearby tree read tailor, but it was unmistakably Laila's house and the local doctor's residence. They knocked on the door, and the girl climbed down and stood on her feet. Her eyes still closed, she yawned and entered the building. "Thanks for taking me home guys," she yawned into the night, and the two disappeared before she shut her mouth.

"Laila! Oh god, not again!" Laila's mother shrieked in horror.

"That's no way for a doctor to walk around. You look like death itself. You gotta stop getting caught in the rain." Her father added.

"It didn't rain today, Dad." Laila's older sister sighed, and a child wailing into the night was the last thing the pair heard before the door slammed shut.

"Well, we need to finish what was started." William began walking back towards the tree.

"You mean go back there?"

"She says if we don't help her, the spell will wear off, and soon."

"Dude, that place gets worse every time we visit."

"I know man, that's why I'll go it alone. We knew the risk of dealing with something like this."

"So what is it she needs anyway?" Jaden posed.

"Essence of fire and the heart of a bear."

"What the living fuck is an essence of fire?"

"I don't even know, man. Let's just focus on the bear. I've seen a couple of bears in the caverns near the forest."

"The forest at this hour?" Jaden's trepidation crept through the question.

"We don't have much time."

"Well, I guess if worse comes to worse, I could do my shadows thing," Jaden said. The bumbling facade quickly being devoured by his malicious, wild eyes and razor-toothed grin.

"Yup, you always can."

"The two went off laughing into the forest,"

"What?"

"Oh, it's nothing.. Just a thing," Jaden remarked.

The two went off into the night with zealous pride. The next morning, Laila awoke in her bed. She wiped the drool from her chin with her pillow... Nope, I'm still mad. Hey, I love a good wake-up routine as much as the next reader, but I'm only human. How about we focus on Mark?

Mark opened his windows with alertness and intensity. He took in the world with vigor and dominance.

"Today's my day!" He shouted into the rest of the village.

"Shut the fuck up, Mark!" Joseph the butcher shot at him, and he fell headfirst from his window. Alright, so maybe Mark wasn't the best focal character... I think Laila's finished getting ready.

Laila dried her face off. She had tried to open the door, but there was a chair placed firmly against it. Now, she just wanted to make sure that she could retain the moisture in her hair. It would be very important for the trials to come. First would come the knock. It would be exactly two knocks because that's the most her mother's patience would allow. She'd reach in with her arms first, which is why it made the most sense for her to face the door so that her hair wasn't pulled. Next would be the tenuous combing, so keeping her hair wet was a good tactic to avoid the other pulling of her hair. After each and every split end was combed out, and Laila's hair was brushed to an inch or two below her shoulder blades, she would finally be released from her clutches as her mother complained loudly about how much she needed to use the bathroom. Spending an extra couple of minutes to return with a wine bottle. There was a point in time when Mei Zhen would hide her vices in a towel or under her robe. She may not have realized it herself, but Laila knew it was about 2 months back when she first forgot to replace the red-stained decanter with a kettle from the parlor room. The parlor room where she spent most of her time drinking *tea*. It was about 3 weeks ago that her mother stopped obscuring the realities of adulthood entirely. Laila returned to her room and threw the clothes laid neatly on her bed into the pile of skirts and blouses that pooled at the side. She put on her usual school skirt and a normal white blouse. She wasn't a fan of the outfit, but she had replaced the uniform top with shirts of a similar design and color. It was something most of the girls on the island and some of the boys knew about that could give their look a little bit of style without drawing too much attention from the teachers. She walked down the stairs, proud of her appearance. Her mother had probably scraped some skin off her head in the process, but her hair looked straight and flowing. This would probably only last until the humidity caught her, so Laila threw her head around as she descended the stairs. "Laila! Can you come here for a second?" She heard her father's loud, authoritarian tone after she was almost at the last step. She sighed.

"No, not really. I got to get to school!"

"I just need an extra pair of hands for two seconds." Her father pleaded.

"Okay, just two seconds, then I'm off to school!" Laila shouted extra loud and made sure to stomp her way up the stairs.

"No! No! No!" Mei popped out of the bathroom, sopping wet, with the suds barely covering her breasts and buttocks. "I just finished washing her hair. You are not going to get it all dirty again."

Mei banged on the door of the doctor's study.

"Sorry, Dad." Laila let out before skipping down the stairs. She opened the door, and in her face was a bearded man. He wore a shirt that looked to be too tight for him thirty pounds ago, and now had his skin spilling from the mid-section. He had stains all along his pants of various sizes and colors. There was a small wagon behind him in which there was a deceased male, and a very stained black cloth over the head.

"Is the doctor in?" The man asked and grinned a smile of mostly missing teeth.

"Dad, someone's at the door for you! He has a wagon!" Laila crossed her arms and shouted into the house, keeping her peripheral vision on the man. Within a few moments, her dad was downstairs, standing tall, wearing a mostly red apron with white splotches from where he avoided staining the garment.

"Joseph, I told you to bring the cadavers to the basement." The Doctor spoke with his arms crossed, and Laila dropped her hands to her side.

"It's not a cadaver, just fell out the window, figured you may be able to stitch him up."

"This man has been dead for at least an hour from the color on his hands. There's also cloth sinking into the clear hole in his skull! Did you shoot this man to use as a cadaver? I told you that's butchery!" The Doctor gestured toward the wagon with his arm.

"Wow, you are good, doc. How'd you figure?" Joseph nodded his head with astonishment.

"Take the hood off for me, Joseph." The Doctor urged. Joseph walked over to the back of the wagon and paused.

"You sure you don't want the little one to go inside? The fall was pretty grisly." Joseph held the covering.

"She's seen worse, and it's good for her to learn these things. She'll be taking over soon enough anyhow." The Doctor looked at Laila, brimming with pride. Laila rolled her eyes, but she kept her sights fixed on the wagon.

"Eh, suit yourself." Joseph shrugged and pulled back the covering. It was a headshot that had pierced the man's head. That was absolutely the killing blow. The fall that shattered his skull, deflating his head like a rubber ball losing air, happened post-mortem. While a grisly scene indeed, her father was correct; she had witnessed worse. It wasn't until her father's breath hitched, and he gasped, holding his mouth, that she realized those may have been horrors that he never found, even in his long medical career.

"Holy shit that's…"

"A lot of blood- that is a lot of blood," Jaden wheezed, coughing up spats of blood as he tried to collect the viscera spilling from his abdomen.

"That bear was surprisingly adept," William observed. The wild animal lunged towards William and stuck its claw through the already mortally wounded Jaden. William jumped back, "I think we need a few more utensils for this quest." Jaden remained unresponsive, paling eyes staring into the distance. The bear was a staggering height, nearly doubling Jaden's length. His body seemed average in comparison with the bear's massive standing structure. Weighing at least 500 pounds, the bear drew its arm back and flung Jaden's body from its claw before charging at William.

"Shit." William ducked under trees and through brush. He grabbed onto branches and made his way into the cavern of disdain and malcontent. He backed out of the cavern and ran into the clearing. The bear followed after, charging furiously at the boy. He turned around and managed to evade the initial charge. He made sure to thump the hide a little so it spun to face him and hit the beast with such precision and force, the only sound that could be heard was the thud of the animal falling in the flowery clearing.

"Aaah!" Jaden came out, clothes torn and bloodied, waving a small branch.

"Where's the knife?" William said, holding his hand out.

"I think it's back in the forest," Jaden recalled. The first attempt to kill the bear did not go as well as he planned. The huge claw-shaped rips across the area of his shirt that should cover his abdomen were overtly clear signs of his inexperience.

"Go get it."

"No, you go get it."

"You're the one who lost the knife," William remarked coldly.

"I know, but I died at least 7 times last night, and it's pretty tiring."

"I killed the damn bear!" William howled.

At that instant, the two felt tall fingers and big masculine hands squeezing their shoulders, throwing them to the floor. It was Shiela Shuckers, the town mayor.

"Whatever you two are doing, stop!" She pinned their heads to the ground and slammed them on the grassy knoll. She peered up at the large bear corpse and lifted the boys by the hair as her surprise rose. "What. Are. You. Two. Monkeys. Doing!" She slammed their heads into the ground with every other word as she reacted to the absurdity of the circumstance.

"We're getting a bear heart and essence of fire!" Jaden blurted out. Shiela shot them each a quizzical look.

"We're getting a bear heart for Sam. He has some pirates from the eastern island, and they have a pretty weird taste." William attempted to smooth over as he spat out dirt.

"Pirates? Haven't you learned yet?" She questioned. "I'm sorry. I know we all lost a lot, but that's exactly why I'm keeping watch of every corner of this island." She instantly got to her feet, "Nothing like that is ever going to happen again, so you boys get back- actually, you two stay here. I'll take care of those pirates." She ran off towards the town.

"Wait, do you have a knife we can borrow?!" Jaden screamed after her. Shiela threw a heavy piece of cloth back at him. "Thank you!" he yelled. "Alright, let's get a move on."

"We still don't have any essence of fire," William added disinterestedly.

"Baby steps," Jaden finished, jamming his blade into the neck of the animal's corpse.

"Laila, how are things in the upper classes? I think I just saw a couple of your classmates by the forest. They were playing with a dead bear..." Shiela proclaimed, resigned.

"Things are going well, thanks, Mrs. Shuckers- did you say dead bear?"

"Yeah, William and the red-haired one who's always with him."

"Ah, okay, that sounds about right,"

Laila continued on her route, and Shiela Shuckers continued bashing in the faces of several visitors from nearby towns she assumed were foreign criminals. She made it a little away from Shiela before a familiarly annoying voice had chimed into her daily stroll.

"Laila was disappointed she was going to school, and school sucked majorly, but she had to go 'cause she's Laila."

"I'm going to hurt you," Laila replied without even turning her head. Jaden appeared out of the brush.

"What is it?" Laila said, still shaking her pent-up rage between a balled-up fist.

"Nothing much, just checking in. Know where Willie is, right?"

"More tasks from her?" Laila questioned, irritated.

"Yeah," Jaden responded quickly.

"Well, that's okay as long as she doesn't have..."

"Have what?"

"Nothing," Laila said quietly, but her hand lingered over her chest and quickening heartbeat. She rushed off downhill and was on her way.

CHAPTER 6

"Say cheese!" Leanna grabbed her daughter by her rosy cheeks and smiled almost as hard as her darling little girl while they tumbled across the meadow. Leanna was a truly beautiful woman whose youth and vitality were perpetually worn. She had long, light-brown, wavy hair that curled around the side of her head in a loose ponytail. Two hazel-green eyes shimmered in the sunlight. Reflecting the natural glisten from her downward-turned lips. Her daughter inherited most of her traits, aside from the eyes. They were a deep cerulean blue.

"Cheesy peesy, man this is easy!" Sarah responded.

"That's still not cheese, bubaboo," Leanna remarked, teasing her daughter.

"Well, Cheese," Sarah said.

"Such a smartypants," Leanna laughed and took hold of her hand. "Where do you find such big words?" Leanna swung her hand with the child.

"My mommy taught me!" she cheered excitedly.

"You must have a really smart mommy, little girl."

"Hey, I'm not a little girl,"

"Oh yeah?" Leanna played along.

"Yeah. I'm a little lady."

"Gasp, a little lady? Already? Felt like yesterday, I was changing the lady's diaper."

They both laughed and sank into the meadow, letting the moment develop.

"Laila!" Sarah shouted out and shot up, sprinting across the field. She jumped into Laila's arms.

"Bubaboo!" Laila said, lifting the child up.

"Where's your mommy?" Laila asked curtly.

"Over there!" Sarah shouted, pointing towards her emotionally fatigued caretaker. Leanna waved slowly from the meadow. She collapsed in the middle of the field, and Laila glared sideways at her. Laila let the child down easy.

"Awww, Bubaboo, I'm sorry you should go to your mommy. I have to be in school soon. I can't play right now," Laila said gently. Leanna shot up like a weed, hands clasped tight, pleading with her younger sister.

"Why do you call me Bubaboo?" Sarah pouted, and she looked up at her young aunt as her lip quivered.

"That's what you wanted to be called. Your mom tried to name you Sarah, and I asked you what name you wanted." Laila gave a playful sternness.

"That's when I was a baby, I couldn't even make words. Now I can say my name, and it's Sarah."

"Okay, Buba- Sarah, you're right, that's so smart. Where'd you learn that?"

"I've been reading a lot, I can say elabo-rate sentences, and I've been expressing my feelings." Sarah proudly turned her nose up and grinned. Leanna shot up once again, mimicking a slap that quickly turned into what seemed to be strangling motions.

"Oh yeah, what books are you reading?"

"Well, it's not a book. William Harvey has a pamphlet on blood *circ-u, circula- circulayme-*." Sarah's neck strained as she closed her eyes and focused on the word...

"Circulation." Laila corrected, but now with a bit of dry agitation. Leanna had begun miming punching whilst still keeping a good grip on the imaginary figure.

"Yeah, Grandpa showed it to me. He said it took you three days to read, and it only took me two and a half." Sarah's pride returned, and she upturned her nose once more.

"Well, did you like it?" Laila lowered her body to meet Sarah's gaze.

"I love learning. What book are you reading now?" Sarah let out with fervor.

"Oh, I haven't picked up a book in a while. I've just been preoccupied- Busy!" Laila simplified.

"I know what *preoppufied* means. You need to be busy reading more books!" Sarah stuck out her tongue, running towards the center of the meadow and tackling her mother to the ground.

"Un-uh," Leanna protested, holding her daughter inches away from her face as the offspring clawed menacingly. "Laila, hold on a second." Leanna managed to strain out and retain her defense.

"I can't babysit right now. I have school."

"You can be a couple hours late and still graduate at the top of your class. Have I taught you nothing?" Leanna sneered, and a rogue claw scratched her cheek.

"You've literally never taught me anything, Leanna, I'm going now." Laila turned.

"Ow! Wait! Ow! Just 5 minutes!" Leanna protested. "Lady Sarah, how about a round of flower crowns?" Leanna asked and watched her daughter's eyes light up as she jumped off to the field and tackled a pile of grass.

"Laila!" Leanna shouted, and Laila reluctantly faced her sister.

"Make it quicker." Laila folded her arms.

"You know Dad's birthday is next week?" Leanna blew a strand of her hair before releasing the band on her ponytail.

"I was not aware of this, no, nor how pressing the detail was," Laila accompanied with an eye roll.

"Watch it. Look, Dad's getting up in age, and I think he's ready to announce you as his new heir." Leanna shook her head and tilted it to gather strands of her hair.

"Do I also get the house or just the responsibilities?"

"I'm serious, Laila. He's going to announce it any day now. His birthday, your birthday, everyone knows you're capable. We're just waiting for you to be ready. Remember Dad-"

"Became the village doctor at thirteen. I've heard the story way more than you. Why don't you have to do it?" Laila's brow furrowed, and some bitterness accompanied the question.

"I got pregnant, and I don't know medicine. Why do you keep denying this? You're like the only one who can be the village doctor."

"Well, maybe I don't want to be in this village! Maybe I don't even want to be on this island!"

"Oh god, Laila, I remember being thirteen too... Is everything okay with you and William?" Leanna had fixed her hair into a tighter ponytail, staring at Laila with that motherly look as if she were a child bawling out after a scraped knee.

"I'm going now." Laila turned around and stormed off. The thoughts of her future swirled around in her head, and the most sickening aspect of the events that would come to pass was how vividly she could imagine them playing out. She gripped tighter to her textbook. It had felt so heavy when she first picked it up, but now she carried it around with ease. Most students carried bags, parcels, or left them in desks. She was the only student to carry a textbook in her arms, which is what all her classmates expected. They couldn't comprehend how unwieldy the book was in her hands despite the ease with which it was held, nor remember any volumes or material she held prior to the textbook. She wanted to stop and debate all the assumptions with her own arguments, but it was no use. Nothing would change. Everything around her felt so familiar and predictable. This is why when Laila saw a familiar but unusual sight in the schoolyard, her eyes lit up, and her thoughts derailed as she ran over to the boys.

"What are you two doing here?" she inquired.

"We're here to see you. How are you, Laila?" Jaden said, plopping himself on the grass.

"You have blood on your pants." Laila pointed out.

"See, there it is, Willie, I told you!" Jaden hopped to his feet, scratching at the stain on his thigh.

"So you're gonna spend the day at-, I mean, by the school?" Laila asked innocently. Shuffling closer to William.

"No," he said plainly. "We were just checking if everything was okay."

Laila kicked his shin in a tendon that caused a piercing pain to run through his leg, where he couldn't help but grab at the site of razzed nerves, leaving the bear's heart to fall to the ground. Crushed as William tried to recover his footing. All the while, Laila ran off into the building, not sparing a glance backwards.

"That was the last bear heart," William growled.

"I'm honestly surprised you got that many bear hearts." Jaden retorted, placing both hands on his carefree head.

"We'll still need that essence of fire. How in the hell do we find that?" William dragged his foot in the dirt, dusting the fatty material from his shoe.

"Why didn't you ask the witch?" Jaden stared blankly. "She's the one who asked you to get it."

"I don't think it's good for me to spend more time than necessary." William rubbed the back of his head and looked off in the distance.

"And you didn't think an explanation was necessary... Look, we don't need to know where to find it, just who knows what it is!" Jaden threw his hands up with enthusiasm.

"And who do you know that I don't?" William looked up at his friend incredulously.

"Never said you didn't know 'em, remember Alicia?" Jaden placed a proud hand on William's shoulder.

"The girl with glasses?" William asked.

"Yeah, her. She's pretty smart."

"You mean she has glasses?"

"Hey, look, there she comes right now." Jaden waved, "Alicia! Alicia! Hey, come over here. We got a question for you."

"What is it?" Alicia pronounced. Alicia had a plain, round face, with no distinguishing features and very leveled cheekbones. Her hair was neatly coiled into a bun. A button nose and tiny eyes that, if pushed closer together, could easily fit upon either side of her face. They were proportional to her round features, however, and even looked wider and full when she wore her eyewear.

"Can you help me get a bit of essence of fire?" he said, staring into her spectacled visage. Alicia widened her stance until she was low enough and, in one fell swoop, knocked Jaden to the floor and continued on her walk. She looked to the ground and shot him a look of abject repulsion.

"Good Day, William." She used two fingers to adjust her glasses before strolling towards the building.

"Hey Alicia," William looked back and forth between the two with confusion, but Alicia gave no pause to even acknowledge a response as she sped into the school. The building itself was rather small for a schoolhouse, but the population had shrunk dramatically after the fire; this is the reason an old repurposed church was enough to hold most of the children on the island.

"Oh god, it's you two," another person suddenly appeared. The two turned to see… Well, we don't know.

"Who are you again?" Jaden Inquired of the mysterious figure.

"I'm Bryce." Bryce was a small boy in height and stature. His face was sharp and pointed, with a diminutive brow that showed his perpetual disinterest. He had a small slouch that hunched his shoulders and hung his uniform over his figure, akin to if someone had hung a coat on a coat rack.

"Bryce?" William grilled the figure. He scanned the recesses of his mind, but he had no memory or recollection of a "Bryce."

"This is one of your jokes, right? I thought you were dead, but I should've known you're just avoiding me." Bryce added in a facetious tone, but the way his voice trembled conveyed the extent of his wound.

"Who hurt you?" Jaden asked. Bryce winced as if he'd been physically wounded. He grasped the tail of his shirt with frustration, balling up the fabric before he let it go, shaking an impulse away.

"You said you'd never forget how I-I-" A small resignation took over the boy, and his frustration dissipated into a deep sigh. "I'm going to school now, appreciate everything that happened and good luck with whatever you're doing now." Bryce made off into the school, not once turning his head to look back at the two.

"What was up with that?" Jaden said, dusting the grass and blood from his pants.

"You sure you don't know that kid?"

"Never seen him," Jaden responded. William shrugged his shoulders, and the two walked off towards the woods.

Alicia walked through the doors with a bit of heaviness. She had slowed her pace, with the slight hope that someone would approach. The moment she made it through the door, she continued on as if nothing was behind her, which had the odd effect of hitting a flustered Bryce in the face. Alicia took no notice. She moved through the halls like a ghost, clutching her books tightly to her person, so they nearly floated through the school. Once she reached the classroom, she turned her head down to avoid the gaze of her peers. They weren't looking at her, even her old group from band practice conversed exclusively amongst each other as she walked past and to her desk. She did want to relay to someone her discomfort, and it wasn't until she spotted the only person in class she could speak with about her troubles.

"Laila!" Alicia whispered, leaning across her desk. "You'll never guess who I just saw. You remember those two kids who dropped out a couple of months ago?"

"I know of them," Laila sighed, and slowly turned to look at Alicia, startled by the seriousness of her expression.

"One of em was my ex," Alicia's chair tilted on its legs as she hovered a little above the seat. Her deadpan expression covered Laila's peripheral as well as immediate view.

"Oh! Your ex?" Laila responded, not wanting to heighten the intensity of the moment, while simultaneously conveying she understood the gravity of this particular encounter.

"That's what I just said, Laila. We were kids, though, so I don't know if it even really counts, but it was the tall one. The tall, dumb, pale one with the long eyelashes and red hair. I was going through a phase. I guess I just really loved red. Anyways, he just, um, propositioned me."

"Wow, like business partners?" Laila shook her head and turned to ask.

"Like partners but not business." Alicia used two fingers to push the glasses up the bridge of her nose.

"Oh!" Laila's eyes widened as she realized the nature of the proposition. "Ohhhh. Ewww."

"I know, right, like he hasn't changed since we were twelve. He's still a dog." Alicia let the chair center and the legs slammed on the floor, bringing her back to her desk. "I wonder who else he's asking that to, jerk," she thought to herself, before throwing her head down in embarrassment.

"Hey Alicia, you okay?" Frannesca leaned over to Alicia's desk.

"What's it to you, Franny?" Alicia picked her head up and questioned with the expression and tone of the frustration that Alicia herself had not even a moment ago tried to bury.

"Whoa, Alicia, I'm just checking in, you seemed a little upset." Frannesca Zimo put her hands up, slowly backing away. Frannesca Zimo was about the same age as Alicia. Her head was topped with long red curls that went down past her shoulders. She always kept an air of propriety about her, walking and sitting with her back perfectly upright. Frannesca put a lot of care into her appearance, making sure to keep her outfits as wrinkle-free as her textbook pages.

"Now you want to check on me, for what? You run out of gossip from people, and now you need to go to the source." Alicia backed her chair out of her desk, and the soft chatter of the classroom silenced.

Frannesca backed away slowly, like a person encountering a large predator. The shock wore off, and upon seeing the agitated state her classmate was in, Frannesca's anger rose to a similar level of frustration.

"I know I've been terrible in the past, but I figure you, of all people, would understand not wanting to be tied down to the way people think about you! Lover girl!" Frannesca extended her finger towards Alicia's face.

"Frannesca, come on, that's a low blow." Dayvonna, a girl who also kept her uniform very pristine and took great care in her appearance, chimed in. Rushing over to hug the agitated redhead.

"You can't let the freaks get to you." Sieya, another girl who was a little less pristine than her associates, but the smudges and stains were close to the top of her shirt and bottom of her sleeves, so this could have been due to makeup, a substance far less gross when recognized. She patted Frannesca's head.

"I know, I know. That's what brings me to their level."

"Just take a walk and breathe." Dayvonna soothed Frannesca with the same patting motions atop her head. Frannesca put both of their hands down. She took an audibly loud inhale and walked a couple paces, but ended up stumbling over Cadence. Cadence was one of the brighter students in the class. Her shirts were always wrinkled, and her skirts never seemed to be the right length. Stopping closer to her thigh than her knee.

"Oh darn, I'm so so-" Frannesca began apologizing until she realized how engrossed Cadence was in the lips of her boyfriend, Guilliam. Another bright student. A boy who had black, wild, quaffed hair much like Cadence. He usually buttoned his shirt up to about his chest and refused to wear a tie.

"Absolutely not! Y'all can't block the whole aisle!" Frannesca reprimanded, sucking her teeth and creating a low-pitched sound with her mouth that sounded like a glass being rubbed clean. Dayvonna hung her head and crouched, trying to remove herself from the situation. Sieya began applying makeup with the implication that this would be the only way she'd be dirtying her hands.

"Like seriously," Saphron added and then curtly ducked her head behind a book. Saphron was a small girl with short, neat, combed hair. She had vibrant green eyes and was the youngest in the class, being born around 10 months after Laila. She usually stayed to herself. Alicia didn't mean to be so closed off, there were several people in the class who had always viewed her as the bubbly, friendly girl. Frannesca was right; she had been far removed from that identity and associated attachments. That was the majority of what she wanted to express, but the words always found themselves muddled in the resentment she held over the class's betrayal. She couldn't just be with them, and to give that bubbly, warm impression, she needed to be able to do just that. She had tried for a while, but the resentment would find its way into gestures, tone, and her word choices. It also delayed the change and created some confusion about Alicia's newly acquired demeanor. Now this reaction from Saphron was something she saw herself in more than the general empty pleasantries and vapid ideas exchanged by her classmates. It was something real she could explore and authentic that she could respond to, she looked over to Laila to gauge her response but she was met with the bushy brown ponytail as her friend stared out of the window of the old classroom, the town in clear view as the people bustled about never carrying a haul too large, and not spending much time at places unobscured. This is what made it much easier to understand. The teacher was once more nowhere to be found. She gazed out, wondering what life would be like if she weren't here, not with them, just not here. The window found its way into her view more than any person or item in the class. She had thought about climbing the trees outdoors, skipping along the path into town, or stopping at a sweets shop until her mind raced, and propagated ideas about the world outside the island. It was much safer to leave it to the imagination, that's why she chose to imagine the world outside from her little window.

Ephriam ran through the village at top speed. He had joked with the students when they were younger that he would personally drag them to class if they skipped more than two lessons. It was a threat he assumed would never need follow-through, as the children of the island welcomed and even appreciated their education. In Ephriam's eyes, at least, but he did understand that his sizable frame and abnormal athletic competence contributed to their compliance. He could also conceive that at his age, he no longer had the spryness to keep up with the children's antics. He kept thinking of his retirement and let that block out all the areas that were usually sore from this much strain. Teaching was a young person's game. In all his years of being an educator, he never had students who intentionally opted out of his lessons. He had practiced wrangling the students of his colleagues, but these were students whom he taught. Ephriam kept up with them for as long as he could, but their hiding spots were getting more creative. He knew there was no way he could keep racing to the haunts, much less discovering their new hideouts. He knew soon he'd be reaching his limit, but before that, he had reached the cavern of disdain and malcontent. The first thing he did was leap to the stalactite hanging from the ceiling. The river crashed and raged all around him, but he kept in his pacing from stalactite to stalactite without skipping a beat. He scaled down the pit of disdain ever so carefully, tying a rope to one of the stalactites of malcontent. Using rocks that stuck out from the wall to make his way down, he adjourned through the dark, cavernous halls and found them. His two idiot former students, trying to set the cave on fire.

"You two are morons," Ephriam interjected. "I can't believe you two right now; I really can't-"

"Stuff it. Essence of fire, do you know of it?" William flung the flint he was holding to the side.

"Whoa, no, I'm an unwed man, William. I haven't known the essence of fire since Sheila's great-great-great-grandmother Senna Falls. Whew. Now she had what it took to light a man's-"

"Okay, so here's what's going to happen: I'm going to punch him hard. Do you want in on that?" William cracked his knuckles.

"How old are you?" Jaden shouted.

"Look, if that's why you two left school, looking for each other's essence, I understand; but listen, you can just tell an adult anytime somebody bothers you. Your friends will understand, and if not, you can always make new friends. You know, meeting the people who accept you for who you are will make your experience all the more valuable. I'm pretty sure you aren't the only ones either. Not sure if I should be saying this, but there's this Bryce kid-"

"Look, dude! We have no idea what essence of fire is! You're a teacher, can't you just teach or something!" William pleaded with the old, balding man.

"Look, boys that's not in my curriculum per se-"

"Okay, I'm gonna hit him," William cracked his knuckles.

"I got your back." Jaden stood up and stretched his forearm.

"Wait! That's exactly what this conversation is. It's much more alchemical. More of a metaphorical fire. Stoking one's essence until they are ablaze. I can't remember the last time anyone used that term. May help to update some of your vocabulary. You know there's a course next year-" The boys were gone, though, they had shimmied up the rope and took it with them. Ephriam looked up at the long passageway and picked up the leftover flint. He struck it against the cave wall, realizing it could be a while before he was rescued. It was a dud, so he struck it once more.

— CHAPTER 7 —

William stood in the witch's den, the heart still warm in his hand.

"This will be the last thing I ask." Those were the words he heard as he carried Laila on his back out of the cabin. The actual request itself was given as his arms were caressed, and they prepared to throw themselves into a steamy passion. William could remember every motion and detail vividly. There was no sadness, nor trickery, not even a playful joke, just two beings led only by desire. Presently, William wished to forget the ordeal entirely. He shifted his bloodied shoes on the dark floor and shook his head. This was the task that would help him gain his humanity back, put the witch and their cabin behind, and allow him to truly love the way he knew, the way he wants, and the way she's been trying to remind him day after day, even after-

"Here." The thoughts in his head became too weighty, and he dropped the heart. A table made of dark material appeared from underneath, cushioning its fall before both table and heart slid like a cart with a crooked wheel directly in the middle of William and the witch.

"Yes Excellent," the witch examined the heart. "I can feel the flames radiating from this one"

"So what now?" William mused.

"Well now we put it in you" The table shot under William. He waited with a blank expression and the black snakes bound his arms in place as the table grew to adjust to his form. "It doesn't have to be a bear y'know" the witch's voice usually relayed too many tones to process any intention but there was something more human that was being presented, almost a fear that overrode the usual dubious nature of their conversations. "Any creature will do all that really matters is you get a burning essence and let's face it bears aren't the only ones who feel a little fire." The buttons of his shirt undid themselves slowly and deliberately, creating a haunting dread as William was disrobed at a pace he could not stall or quicken, only watch. The tails of the button-down draping the sides of the table, like the fabric of a robe parting before an offering. The lining of his scar began to burn as a warm, incendiary tongue ran across the ridges.

"Can you just focus on the task at hand?" He answered, annoyed with the salacious focus on his scar.

"Hold your horses it's a process" the bear heart dripped over William's scar, and the thin, icy fingers squeezed the organ until it discolored. The lining where William's scar was melted, leaving his chest cavity open and exposed to the darkness. It twisted and turned around the area until the bear's heart had vanished from the room entirely. His heart remained black and twisting, his chest cavity sealed itself up after the procedure had been finished, and William opened his eyes and sat upright, gasping for air. He looked into the witch's cool diamond eyes and looked to the ground. He put his hands in front of him to make certain he hadn't been tied down.

"That can't be right There should have been at least some adjustment" Icy fingers made the hair on his skin stand as they felt his chest. "Nope kid looks like I was wrong you're still not alive"

"Don't give me that, you said we needed to kill a bear while it was mating. Do you have any idea what that was like? How can I still be dead?"

"Okay first of all non-living doesn't mean dead A rock isn't alive or dead" William stared, arms crossed against his chest. There was the fear again, it was brief but the rushed pronunciation showed a trepidation William scant experienced in the cabin in anyone other than himself, but there was something more to this moment, something hidden, something the witch was trying to protect. "Look I'm sorry I thought there'd be enough fire in an animal as big as a bear You need a higher heat signature Bring me anything with a blazing fire and I swear your humanity will be returned to you."

"So an elephant?"

"Elephants don't love too much they remember a whole bunch but their fire burns low."

"So a humpback whale?" William naively inquired.

"I'm talking more along the lines of your little friend"

"Jaden's what got us into-"

"That's not who I meant and you know it hun"

William gritted his teeth and clenched his fist; everything became still in that moment, even the twisting darkness. Brilliant diamond eyes mirroring the celestial wonders of the nighttime shore looked into his strained expression and began, "Now that fire that flame was truly spectacular" The cackles echoed across the room, as a roaring fire appeared behind them, unlike any fire ever seen. The color was black, and while it crackled and flared the same, this particular tinder carried a more sinister aura. The dark flame shone, but the brightness emanating from it was not what made it so blood curdling, but instead the ever-twisting, ever-changing animation that dared onlookers to look on, with the promise that if they'd turn their back for even a second, their soul would be forever lost to the abyss.

"This was a mistake. You said this would be the last time. We're done." William hopped off the table and headed towards the door.

"Wait" the Witch bellowed after him. "Don't you want to be human again to feel the warmth of a friend's happiness or the raging fury of your own anger" A tender voice followed him down the hall, pleading, but William was finished. He had enough of the tricks and misdirections, he barely cared what the witch was hiding anymore. It could very well just be another waste of time anyway. "What about the excitement of new love!" The witch screamed, fist balled behind their back, and William stopped in his tracks. "Listen there is one other way you can become human but it's not proven to completion it could end in even more misery than you've endured in the first place" William sighed deeply, and the dark, ethereal form coiled around him. "There's one other way but it could twist the very fabric of reality Unleash a series of catastrophes that forever alter this plane"

"The fuck are-"

"Would you see to the end of this world"

"If that's the world that will see us together."

"You are the truth, aren't you" the witch cackled. "I swear one day that blaze will be mine"

William turned his head.

"Have you ever heard of a little thing called the zodiac?"

— CHAPTER 8 —

"So you have to kill all 13 animals?"

"Consume." William answered.

"So what was the bear heart for?"

"I don't know- experience, I guess."

"I could have skipped that experience." Jaden hopped off the steps, gathering himself. He ran his hands frantically over his torso and chest before relaxing his arms at his side.

"It has to be the animal."

"What do you mean?" Jaden stared up at William as he crouched to fiddle with something on the ground.

"Those original 12 animals all did exist, and they've passed down their status from generation to generation."

"So we have to kill the 12 magical animals of the zodiac. Well, this makes a lot less sense now." Jaden got up from the floor, and the fiddling turned out to be the decapitation of a small hare. "Lucky rabbit's head,"

"That's foot. And the alternative is more mating bears." William said, and Jaden tossed the severed head casually into the forest.

"I don't know if there are any bears left to mate. Does it have to be all 12, and can't you just knock em out, why kill em?"

"The witch said consume." Jaden grimaced at the words. "The only way to do that is to become Man. Man is the master of beasts. The only way to become Man again is to master all the beasts. Don't worry, I got us into this mess, and I have felt weirdly hungry since the last check-up." William flashed a small grin, but it only elicited a worry from Jaden that was quickly masked by his bright-teethed playfulness.

"Well, some of those may not be in this town or even the world. Actually, I don't think dragons have existed for a while."

"Okay, we don't need to do the dragon first. Let's start with something small like the pig."

"You mean the random pig that could be at any point in the universe?"

"Come on. I have a good feeling about this."

William and Jaden ran off onto the cobblestone path with more fervor than their usual effort, and they swept through the town, avoiding Sam, Joseph, wells, stairs, fences, and other structures. Still, somehow, Jaden bumped into Alicia.

"Oh god, of course it's you," Alicia said, falling to the floor. She hit with a thud, her glasses flew off, and for a moment, they landed a little ways away, completely untouched, not even a scratch on the lens. Usually, Alicia would have been well into the woods by the time Bryce made his way to the town square. Instead, he saw Jaden and Alicia sitting on the floor, he hopped back, hearing a crunch but barely paid it any notice. Watching from the corner, wishing to be on that grass in front of those tall legs. He looked towards his timid feet, and saw he stood on the girl's glasses. The lens was shattered, and the frame was nearly flattened. So there was really no harm to give it a couple extra stomps.

William went on running, thinking of his humanity. He was smart enough to know how to respond to different social situations, but when he ran through the crowded town square at unusually high speeds, it really made him contemplate which expression he should be using. At the moment, he went for his usual clean, unconcerned look. He took off at top speed over the hill; he was confident enough in his movements to keep his mind active. He went across to the other side and down the dirt path to the back of the old church.

"I'm telling you they're broken." Alicia, still on the ground with her arms folded, looked outwards as far as she could, squinting into the distance. Jaden hurriedly searched the floor for her eyewear.

"I heard the crack, just go. I'm sure I'll find my own way. I basically memorized the route." Alicia tried to use her fingers to adjust her glasses and nearly poked her eyes.

"It's alright. I can take you. I was kind've headed there anyway."

"Oh are you both finally coming back to school?" Alicia looked off to the side. She could barely see him, but she didn't even want him thinking he received any of her attention even if it was peripheral.

"No, just to the building, I've been there a couple times already." Jaden scratched his head and smiled an awkward grin as Alicia stumbled to her feet, and dusted herself off, blushing with embarrassment.

"I'll be going now," she shuffled off into the crowd before Jaden could say a word. He got up and searched for her. He pushed past a group of people, hoping to cut her off before she left the square. He had reached the point before realizing she no longer lived in that direction. Jaden looked over the crowd, and people seemed to either move away or express their displeasure.

"Hey!" A person yelled out, and Jaden slithered through the crowd, but it was too late. He couldn't get a sight, nor a hint of Alicia.

"Standing as high as some tree branches, the beast of the forest is this island's indomitable force. None can slay nor train the beast, and as with all forces of nature, the island's inhabitants would form a harmony by using its ferocity to guide the borders of the villages inland." Ephriam paced around the front of the classroom, didactically reading the book's contents.

"Laila, how long has it been since you've seen Sydney?" William questioned her from the bush.

"I saw her in May, but it's been a while," she leaned over to the window with the book upright.

"Sydney?" Jaden hopped along, "but Sydney is a-"

"Prickly brown fur, powerful hind legs with hooves capable of bracking- bricking- breaking. That should be breaking." Ephriam walked over to his desk and pulled out a quill to make the note.

"Yes, the original was a boar." William pulled Jaden to the floor.

"I was gonna say gu-"

"Laila, meet us by the meadow after class, something I gotta tell you."

"Why can't you-" Laila stood slightly, using the desk to lift herself from her chair.

"Laila!" Ephriam yelled, throwing a book that hit the book standing on her desk.

"What are you?" Laila stared up at Ephriam, who looked out the window at William and Jaden, both crouched under the frame.

"Class, excuse me for one second." Ephriam bowed, posing curtly. CRASH! William and Jaden looked on as the man got up, barely bloodied, the shards of glass sticking out of his skin, like splinters, instead of ripping his muscle tissue. Jaden and William looked at each other and were in agreement; they no longer had to be there. They went off, bounding up the hill. Ephriam got up and gave chase, and everyone in the class once again lamenting the loss of their teacher.

"Ephriam's really getting up in age, huh?" Kerwin closed the portion of the window that still existed.

"Could just be jumping through enough windows," Susanna observed.

"It's the fifth window this year." Anthony grumbled, grabbing a dustpan.

"Hey, does anyone have any gum?" Chesney Adams asked the class.

Anthony and Kerrigan swept up the glass shards. This is a practice they were not only accustomed to but had been made habitual. Kerrigan's father usually did construction on the buildings in town, and as he supported his father's business, he tried to lessen the workload anyway he could. Anthony had lived in a household where he was responsible for taking care of his own mess, which he often found included the messes of house guests, his siblings, and his parents when they were overworked. The only exception being his cousin Kerwin, who made japes the entire time but pitched in with the housework nonetheless.

"We need to stop cleaning up this school's mess. Ephriam's not even paying us. Let's strike!" Kerwin took the broom from Anthony and held it in the air as a symbol of defiance.

"Kerwin, clean up the glass before it go in someone foot." Susanna nearly flung her chair, leaning over her desk to yell, moving her head slightly to avoid directing her ire at Cadence, who skipped over to Guilliam's seat and plopped herself in his lap. She whispered something into his ear, and shortly after, he cleared his throat.

"Hey, Saphron, we're doing a picnic by the pond, you should come." Guilliam offered, and Cadence lit up with pride.

"I have archery later, but maybe after." Saphon smiled, and her teeth ground slightly. Cadence rolled her eyes. She and Guilliam led each other out of the room by their hands, and Saphron stuck her tongue out in disgust, before surveying her surroundings and ducking into her textbook.

"A picnic sounds nice." Laila let out with meek jealousy.

"It does. It really does. I've skipped practice for less. You could bring some nice snacks." Alicia picked up on the sentiment.

"A nice blanket." Laila looked over with the same excitement.

"Nice scenery." Alicia raised her eyebrows.

"Nice far away location." Laila's eyes trailed off into the distance.

Why isn't she going to the picnic?" Alicia slammed the desk, and Laila jumped as she was jolted out of her reverie,

"Can't say. Why don't you ask her after practice?" Laila breathed slowly, calming herself.

"Oh, I always leave early, and she always comes late. Hear this, she's usually late hanging out with Cadence and Guilliam, but she just blew them off. What gives?"

"Why don't you just stay late and ask her?" Laila inquired.

"I can't stay late! I wouldn't get home until way after dark. I live two whole towns away now!" Alicia perked her head up before dropping her chin on the desk after a brief tinge of embarrassment.

"Oh yeah, I forgot you moved a couple months back, and you walk all the way to this part of the island?" Laila rolled her eyes and squinted as she thought of the strain from lengthening her own commute. "Why do you still go to this school?" Laila asked and immediately became concerned about the interpretation of the question. "I mean-"

"For my friends," Alicia admitted plainly. She looked at the back of Laila's head; her hair hadn't been ponytailed for a while, but it was cared for now, and she used more tenderness in her movements. Delicacy in her gestures. Just as the thought crept into her head, Alicia turned away as if someone had caught her gazing, "If you want, you can come, you're always welcome, y'know." Alicia said, patting the back of her hair, "It's about 2 miles past Odette's by the big willow tree, the one that looks like Ms. Donner after she gets caught in a rainstorm." The words felt weird as they hadn't been spoken since the move. It wasn't the inattention of Laila, but that probably hadn't added to her confidence. Feeling an inescapable sinking feeling of dread creeping up the back of her throat, Alicia slammed her face into the crevice of her elbow. Laila smiled at her friend and looked out the shattered window frame before tapping Alicia's desk.

"Pst."

— CHAPTER 9 —

William and Jaden paced themselves after they saw that they had made it far enough.

"So what's the deal? Laila doesn't get out for a couple of hours," Jaden prodded.

"Hey!" Laila said, pulling someone's hand uphill.

"Laila!" Jaden yelled excitedly. He saw the hand she was pulling on, and his face paled, despite being the one uphill. Jaden ducked and fell to the floor.

"Guys, this is Alicia," Laila pushed the plain girl to the middle of the crowd. Jaden got up from the floor, and the four children stood poised awkwardly on the hill.

"Hey.." Alica responded bashfully

Fragments of her glasses still lay around the town square, so she could hardly see where she was going, much less who was there.

"Hello, nice to meet you." Jaden opened, disguising his voice.

"Oh no, not again."Alicia's face dropped. She attempted running off but only bumped into Laila.

"Be nice." Laila shot Jaden a spiteful look that could pierce souls.

"Hi Alicia," he said in an attempt to refresh the situation.

"I get you guys are doing like a thing or a bit, but there's something we gotta take care of, isn't that the reason you two snuck out at lunch?" William began walking down the hill, and the rest followed.

"I snuck out to hang out with Laila," Alicia replied simply.

"You know Chesney still has a crush on you Laila, bet he wouldn't mind hanging out," Alicia teased.

"Yeah, but William actually invited her," Jaden replied.

"Yeah, okay, but Chesney is actually really sweet and not to mention hot," Alicia giggled, her giddiness and charm were beginning to rub off on everyone. They began to go over more of their classmates, making various observations and jokes. They slowed their movements, and for a while, the townspeople were nearly fooled into thinking four ordinary teenagers walked the public in daylight. They finally reached it, the old part of town that remained charred and warm. The blackened doors leading into the dilapidated frames of houses.

"The fire..." Alicia announced, drained. The rest of the children were silent; they hurried to the slope at the end of the old part of town. The ground had been burnt, and the path was rocky. They climbed down the hillside, being very careful not to move too fast and tumble down the deadly slope. The moss-covered rocks proved to be a difficulty for Alicia as she slipped when grabbing one. She fell halfway down before being caught by William. Her breathing increased rapidly, and she shivered at the thought of what was almost to come. Jaden and Laila both jumped off the rocks and gracefully landed.

"That was a close one." Jaden paused in his tracks to check for any damage that might have befallen Alicia, but William's catch had proved one of heroism as the girl was completely unscathed. The moment Alicia caught her breath, she wriggled out of William's arms, startled. She scrambled to her feet and continued on walking.

"Hey, I think this might be the first time you've saved me." Alicia patted herself, still in disbelief that there was not a welt nor scrape on her skin.

"C'mon, now we've known each other for like ten years." William rolled his eyes at the comment.

"I had no idea you all knew each other that long." Laila looked between the two.

"Of course, we were in the same class." Alicia kept her eyes on the rock, but closed her eyes and stumbled when she reached the next stone.

"Alicia, what are you saying? We used to go on adventures all the time after school." William looked back at Alicia as she made it to the small incline, and everyone walked down.

"That wasn't me, that was Cadence." Alicia laughed.

"It definitely was Cadence, dude." Jaden agreed, and Alicia and Laila's breathing slowed as they stared daggers at him, "What? *It was Cadence!*" They all came to the front of the old school. They had been to the building all throughout their youth and almost held an expectation on their path. The fence still remained upright, but the rest of the building was charred beyond comparison. There were no windows that hadn't been entirely blackened if not completely shattered. There were still some piles of rubble lying around the inside, but their desks, chairs, and even the bathrooms had been reduced to ash. The rubble was likely a combination of the ceiling and the wall; any semblance of their schoolyard days had been lost or radically disfigured.

"The old school," Jaden whispered.

"Where?" Alicia questioned.

"It's right there between the rubble and the ash, are you blind- oh wait." They continued on along the side of the building until they had reached a large open field next to a forest.

"Laila, do you think you can bring Sydney out here?"

"Oh, of course! I've been waiting to introduce her to you!" Laila nearly jumped into the air. "Sydney! Sydney!" Laila called into the forest, "Sydney!" She called out, walking into the brush. "So whose Sydney?" Alicia asked.

"He's Laila's pet pig," William responded coldly.

"What?" Alicia responded, baffled. William walked to what used to be the back entrance of the old school. There were a couple of stairs that remained intact. They were not burnt but were covered in soot, the original material for building the steps nearly unrecognizable. He sat down on the bottom stairs, closed his eyes and relaxed his muscles.

"Sydney's not her actual pet," Jaded contributed. "They met a couple of years back. Sydney was being attacked by poachers in the forest when along came Laila and-"

"She stopped the poachers?" Alicia asked excitedly.

"No," Jaden replied, laughing, "she distracted them long enough for Sydney to…"

"Sydney to what?" Alicia pressed.

"To deal with them, but like a half-off deal because they were cut in half." Alicia felt the horror grow in her chest, and her eyes paled.

"My god…" Alicia looked to the steps where Willian meditated and back to Jaden, who picked his nose.

"You're all just doing nothing! Laila's in there alone!" Alicia shot past Jaden into the forest. Alicia had no ready plan of action, but she assessed that it was better than sitting around doing nothing. Although without her glasses, she could hardly do a thing. She didn't dare turn back, despite being only a few inches away from the clearing, she dove through the forest and went deeper and deeper until she came to a river. Well, she believed it was a river. She couldn't see much but the moist, soft soil she stood on. The sound of water rushing and crashing against rocks led her to a very safe assumption. She kneeled down onto the bank, extended her hand and sipped some of the cool liquid. Today had definitely helped her work up a thirst; she'd never admit it, but her legs ached and her hands were cut from grabbing so tightly onto the rocks. Alicia knelt over the water and squinted at her reflection. Her hair was messier than usual, there were dirt marks on her cheek, and one of her eyes went red from straining to view her appearance. She dunked her face in the river and opened her eyes to see a singular salmon as it sped upstream. She lifted her head up to see it jump, and then grabbed it right out of the air by a powerful set of jaws. Alicia leapt back into the stream. It was shallow, and only her skirt had really been soaked until a great splash drenched her entire person.

William sat meditatively on the stairs, and Jaden hopped up. "They sure are taking a while." Jaden bit the flesh from the tip of his thumb and spat it out on a nearby patch of grass. "I knew I should never have let her go by herself; she could barely get down the hill." Jaden fumed, circling the clearing, "Who knows what could happen in there? Where's Laila? It's been too long."

"Well, there is the chance Alicia found him first," William calmly returned to his state of relaxation and sat completely still.

"Dammit, I know-" Jaden's heart raced back and forth, "I'm gonna gut that pig, just you wait!" Jaden yelled, his voice bouncing off the forest. At that moment, the beast came skulking from the forest. Jaden's vision blurred, and he grew weak in the limbs. The animal's tusk gleamed red as it charged them, furious and raging.

Laila continued walking through the brush. It was easier to know the area and not the destination, as she had memorized the area well. A shortcut to get to the old library. She picked herself up and combed the area of the forest, thoroughly searching for the pig. She sighed, looking on. The river was a distance away, and the sun's position implied it was getting late. She sighed deeply and turned around to feel the hot breath across her face. She looked into the eyes of the beast and smiled, "Sydney!" she yelled with elation and hugged the beast that was more than tripled her size by the neck, rubbing her face in its mane. Sydney sat down with a thud that scared the birds out of the trees, but Laila remained stationed in the warmth of her furry friend.

"There's someone I want you to meet." She held the beast by one of its hairs, leading it through the forest. "When'd your fur get so matted?"

The clearing was splashed with blood, the beast lay dead, its own tusk having impaled it, and Jaden pounded his chest, hollering with anger over the big, dead animal carcass.

"There's no heart!" Willie called out. Hands surprisingly clean, for someone who had been rummaging through the innards of a dead boar. "There's actually nothing. How is this possible?!" William stood up and gathered himself. He looked over the animal to find some manner of explanation, but as he returned to make another lap, the body ignited and burned, leaving no trace of the animal whatsoever. The ground where the animal lay looked completely untouched, aside from a few crushed weeds and the blood splattered across the field. There had been no sign of a fire. Jaden remained upright and fuming. William took his seat by the old stone steps and waited with his eyes closed. The field had become eerie, and he needed to focus on the task at hand, not jumping to any conclusions or assumptions. He sat and meditated, trying to clear his mind and figure out his surroundings, although he did not concentrate too much on the latter. Jaden sat back, his eyes still panicked. He tilted his head back and stared up at the sky. It was the only thing that made sense, that he absolutely knew was there. He tried not to think of Alicia and what had become of her; he wanted to leave the forest immediately. His stomach turned, and he crouched in pain as the clouds rolled by, "It's getting dark," he murmured to himself. The sun looked almost fixed in the sky; it was as if time itself had come to a standstill, making Jaden's pain worsen. His head had become heavy with thoughts he could no longer stand, so he charged into the forest, leaving William by himself meditating on the blackened stone steps. He bumped into something; luckily, there was a log behind him, which he could rest upon. Unluckily, this was the same log that tripped him onto his behind. He looked up to see the huge, fearsome creature staring him down; he would not be caught off guard this time. He sprang to his feet and took hold of the creature's tusk. He wrestled and tussled with it before it would send him soaring through the forest. Jaden got up, his posture hunched over, and his legs wobbling like a nascent deer. After a very brief moment, he shoved the animal's back hard as his injuries would allow. It was then he saw the plain girl fly off the animal and collide with the log headfirst. "Ow." was all he heard as he rushed to her aid.

"Alicia! Oh my god, you're alright!" Jaden tried to hug her, but she pushed him away and grabbed her head.

"What happened?"

"You've been gone for hours, we thought Sydney got you."

"Got by who? Not Sydney, they're a complete sweetheart." Alicia shook off her incredulity.

"Where were you?" Jaden inquired of the plain girl with the mild head injury. She stood up, still rubbing the area where her head had impacted.

"I don't remember.." she replied, perturbed.

"Just messing with you," she put her hand up to pet the animal, who hadn't moved since her fall. It merely stared down Jaden with an overwhelming murderous intent. She climbed atop him and lay down, looking at the blue, cloudless sky.

"By the river. That's where I met them. I was off washing up when they appeared next to me and scared the living daylights out of me. I fell in the river, and they jumped in. I looked up and I swore I could see them smile, so we laughed and played in the river for a while. I told them who I was waiting for, and I think they understood. They showed me to a pile of their mushrooms, and I guess I must've fallen asleep." She laughed, shooting Sydney a reassuring glance, before burying herself in their furry hide.

Sydney had lived an entire life of indolence. One of the mystical animals of the Chinese zodiac, they had chosen a mammalian form. This gave Sydney a beast-like appearance, nearly quadrupling the size of a normal animal, to about the size of a pygmy elephant. They couldn't remember their birth. It seemed like the island was always home. As far back as the creature could remember, they had been in a manner guarding the forest, and more importantly, the river of the island. Exploring the bounds within reach and the resources in the surrounding parameters. It was during one of these routine excursions that they saw a human girl, who seemed for the most part harmless. Humans usually knew better than to venture into their territory; still, it was nice to be of use to some humans. Some were kind and gave treats, and more than that, thought and understood things so radically different that it was easy to forget that they were all the same species. Well, one human. The visiting human girl had leaned down to the river, and she squinted, brushing her hand across the surface. The way the girl's eyes were so strained, Sydney could clearly see she was readying to wash away an irritant. Sadly, her small, undeveloped human arms could only brush against the water. Sydney had no hands to scoop either, and there

being no humans in the proximity, took it upon themselves to help. They got briefly distracted by a salmon leaping from the river, but even as they crunched down the bones, they offered their assistance. Splashing in the river to help her grab the water.

"Those could have been poisonous," Jaden remarked.

"I trust Sydney." She answered, ruffling their mane. Sydney got on their hind legs, switching their body away from Jaden. Sitting down so Alicia could get a proper mount.

"You want me to get on your back?" Alicia asked with a high-pitched whine and a tear forming in her eye. Sydney thudded themselves on the ground, and the agreement was understood.

"I guess I'll lead the way." Jaden guided the pair towards the clearing.

"So did Laila ever come back?" Alicia asked. This time staring at Jaden from atop the massive boar.

"No, but it's getting dark. She should be back by now."

"Aroooooooooooooo!" Alicia and Jaden instantly turned their heads towards the noise. A large, mangy, wild dog ran charging at the boar and tore into their side. The animals of the forest usually knew their place, but there were a couple of times they got rowdy. Most often ravenously hungry, with the appetite to devour even their own salvation. This wasn't usually a problem, aside from some teeth marks and a couple scratches. The strands being gripped at the top of Sydney's head brought the realization that this was not a solo venture. The boar rose up in pain, and Alicia held tight to the hairs.

"Another one." Jaden turned in time to hit the dog square in the nose, sending it yelping back into the trees. The boar took off for the clearing, and the canines followed in hot pursuit. Through the trees and underbrush, charging. Making wide turns and kicking up dirt. Jaden tried to keep pace, but the boar's movements were splendid, flawless even with the speed it traveled. It rushed for the river, the only sanctuary it could find. There was a pack of dogs now, and they were gaining on Sydney, who turned around and thrust one of them airborne, sending it through the trees. Sydney stared down the two predators that faced them and slowly moved around the animal, being careful to leave not a single opening. Then, out of the corner of its eye, the dog saw the dirtied fist gripping tightly to the fur. It jumped immediately for its chance. The boar slammed its tusk into the creature and halved it. The lone animal took one final horrified glance at its pack member, and as it sat petrified. The ground below it slowly began to muddy as the moisture rose up from the soil. Before it could even turn its head, the jaw slammed directly into the mud as it whimpered, dissolving into the muck.

"Don't worry, Sydney, I got you!" Jaden came waving another random branch from the bushes. He tripped over a log and fell, looking at the halved beast. He rose up in horror. "AHHHHH, what the hell is that?" The boy tripped at the sight of the grisly slicing and backed into the trees.

"Nice job, Sydney." William came out of the bushes, clapping.

"Laila!" Alicia shrieked, "You guys saw all that?"

"Yes, very impressive." William leaned on the tree and yawned. Sydney got up on his hind legs, and Alicia hopped off.

"They're so amazing," Alicia hugged Sydney once more, then ran to Laila's side.

"So which one is this?" William scrutinized, pointing with his finger.

"I think they're all her." Laila scratched her head.

"No, I mean the first one was fire, that one was water- Which one do you think?" William turned to Laila. Sydney froze in horror, their eyes dilated and went in and out of focus. Before Sydney knew it, they had stiffened their hind legs, and their front feet were perfectly still. The grass dancing from the aggressive nostril flaring. The bodies had disappeared, but the scent and even the pain still lingered.

Jaden put his arm over Alicia, and she instantly put it down. Rage swirled around and clouded Sydney's head and vision with a red blur. They charged at William, who had deflected enough bear claws to deftly keep on either side of the charge. William leapt back and chambered his arm as he loaded a palm strike towards the animal. When he released the attack, it delivered a crunch to the chest of the pig, and the beast fell in the middle of the woods. A couple of moments passed, and the beast stumbled to its feet.

"That shouldn't happen." William attempted to leap backwards, but it was too late, and the boar's head whipped around, launching William off his feet and into a nearby tree.

Laila kept pace past the plain girl, and all Alicia could do was watch. The boar charged at Laila, the hind legs the size of a German Shepherd. It briefly paused as a glint of metal shone across its eye. It arced its body upwards, ready to charge, watching William, who had hardly faltered after hitting the tree. He got on his feet, grinning satisfied as a dark, deceitful aura seeped through his teeth. He charged at Sydney and leapt, delivering a devastating blow with the heel of his shoe to the boar's snout. Laila pulled out the knife, the handle almost shaking out of her palm. Sydney quickly turned his head, but Willim had anticipated this and held to one of his tusks. This time, William dug his toe into the animal's neck. It shook its head in a frenzy and sent William sliding towards a tall oak tree. Vines wrapped themselves around his arms as he thrashed against the trunk. Sydney roared a powerful reverberation until fire emitted from the sound and materialized into a pig next to them. The earth began to rumble, and a stream appeared from the ground, bubbling like a geyser until another pig materialized over the crack. The third came from the moisture in the air, coalescing into a vapor that steamed its attributes into existence. There were now four pigs in the field, though their appearances differed slightly. The first pig to materialize had a much lighter coat than Sydney and the rest. The second pig's fur was very matted and tangled. The third pig looked oily and smooth, as if it had no fur.

"Oh no, we have to do something, I think Sydney's been cursed!" Alicia exclaimed with terror.

"Which one?" Jaden replied wide-eyed. The boars roared at the same time, and Alicia was forced to cover her ears.

"Could use a little help." William now flexed his muscles, foregoing escape and only attempting to maneuver the vines. Jaden rushed over, clawing at the restraints and pulling William. Laila appeared in front of Sydney, her hair frenzied by the wind as she held the knife-like comb. The boar could see she was maybe a second or two away from dropping it. Still, the mere resolution she held to protect this boy was lethal. It occurred to Sydney at that moment that this could be the culmination of a beast's existence. Possibly, this was a death more fitting than they deserved. The past trails tread, and the future paths to lead wouldn't actually make a difference in this cruel, unchanging world. A world unbefitting of even a beast. The stars seemed to look down on their fate, but maybe some aspect of it could still lend themselves to the youth. Transcending Beastdome and humanity in one fell swoop, Sydney charged towards the knife, and the boar's neck was ripped open by the only potential they could acknowledge. Alicia fell to the floor and gasped in horror. Laila's hand still trembled, but not with adrenaline. It was anticipation. She knew the cut wasn't clean enough to be immediately fatal, but would be undeniably lethal.

"Laila.." Alicia whimpered. She crawled over to where Sydney lay impaled and looked into their eyes. There was a quiet relief; they looked almost at peace with the clouds reflecting in their beady black eyes. Sydney could feel the last breaths of air filling their lungs and took one last glance at Laila, who walked over, holding the knife head turned towards the ground.

"You don't need to see this." Jaden rushed to Alicia's side in moments, covered her eyes and turned her around. Laila watched the light fade from her friend's eye. She wanted to walk back, but she knew the knife had dug in far too deep. She wanted to cry, she wanted to yell and grab some thread to patch the wound, but she knew it was far too late. She would only prolong the animal's suffering. She caressed the corner of Sydney's jaw.

"GRRRRRRRRRRMMMMMMM!" The animal let out a blood-curdling scream as Laila dug into the neck.

"GRRRRMMMM!" they let out once more, less stirring, now more aggravating for Laila as her hands became coated while she ruptured major veins.

"Grmmmmmmm.." Sydney groaned slightly before their eyes rolled into the back of their head, and Laila dropped the knife with a clink on the moistened dirt. William walked next to the dead boar and kicked it as it lay unresponsive and lifeless. His pupils shrank to dots as his iris lit up with malice, and his teeth sharpened and pointed, resembling a bear trap. Then the dark appendages grew. Darkness that could taint the nature of any man's soul. They tore into the boar, feeding it to the boy, ripping the carcass piece by piece and shoving it into his mouth, shredding the morsels on his razor-sharp teeth, until the boar was all devoured and nothing remained but the halved wolf lying by the river bed. William felt a surge of disgust teeming in his stomach. He leaned over the tall oak tree and crumbled to his knees. He hadn't heard anything but his sinister deeds in the silent forest. The chewing and swallowing of such horror. His head spun around, and he swooned, caught by Laila, who proceeded to pet his head. She let the boy gently onto the floor, placing his head on her lap as Alicia sobbed, being held by Jaden. At that point, it didn't matter what time it was, where they were, or what had happened. They were all true and honest to their nature in that brief moment in the forest. Alicia struggled out of Jaden's grasp and immediately punched him. She looked in horror at the field and how nothing remained of her friend. Laila looked up at her with pale, blank, expressionless eyes, which hit such an unbelievably stomach-wrenching pang of guilt that prompted Alicia to run off alone into the forest.

"It's dark. She'll surely die if you don't go after her," Laila petted William's head. He stared up at her with the same blank, emotionless eyes that she did him, and it was there, with only the moonlight to realize each other, that they had found truth. Jaden got up and ran after Alicia, who hadn't made it very far before tripping and sobbing uncontrollably.

"I don't understand," Alicia tried to gather herself. Jaden helped her to her feet,

"I'll take you home."

"No! I need an explanation. What was that? Why'd you guys-" Alicia fell to her knees and started tearing up. "Why'd Laila?"

"Love."

"What?" Alicia said, her face twisting with incredulity.

"William, well, there was an accident a while back, and he, well, he doesn't feel emotions anymore."

"What do you mean? I saw the sick bastard smile before Sydney got-"

"Yeah, about that no."

"What do you mean no?"

"Well, he can imitate emotions, he isn't stupid."

"What are you saying?"

"Laila is trying to save William. Just like he saved me." Jaden bowed his head and raised his arms in a martyr-like pose.

Alicia stared at the boy, insulted beyond disbelief, her expression of disdain quickly growing into fury.

"What?" Her confusion had quickened her breathing, and she struggled to keep her head straight.

"There was this curse placed on us by a witch because I died after the village fire, and Willie went to the witch's forest to revive me that night, but she made him give her his heart in exchange for hers, and I became a shadow."

"What?!" Alicia grew tired of Jaden's frustration. "So William's heart belongs to the witch, and William has the witch's heart, and you're a shadow?"

"That just about sums it up."

"That's the most ridiculous thing I've ever heard in my life."

"What's so ridiculous?"

"Jaden, I'm leaving," she turned around, tripping over a log, and Jaden laughed heartily and strong.

"Ughhhh, you suck. But that actually felt like you." She groaned as Jaden helped her up.

"Priceless." Jaden wiped a tear from his eye. He relished in the humor until the sentiment was processed.

"Wait, what?" Jaden asked, but Alicia did not turn back to acknowledge him. She only turned after misjudging directions enough to follow Jaden's lead to the clearing.

— CHAPTER 10 —

Alicia got up early in the morning. She stretched and stood before falling into her bed on her back. She lay, looking at the white ceiling, a blank canvas for her imagination. She shuddered at all that was running through, all that had happened when her eyes closed. She attempted to remove her glasses, but then remembered their condition and shoved her face in a pillow.

"I mean, it's not like I have anything better to do," she thought aloud. It was true. Upon seeing the vicious state she returned in, Alicia was in quite the predicament.

"What is that god-awful smell?" She could hear her father's voice from outdoors. He shuffled around the foyer, and her mother was the first to open the door.

"It's Alicia, dear." Her mother held her nose.

"Alicia, where the hell were you?" Her father rushed to the front.

"I just got a little lost heading home. Can I come in now?" Alicia whined, her legs nearly trembling from the weight of her journey and shivering in the chilly night.

"Not so fast." Alicia's father put out his hand. "Heading home from where? And before you try it, I already talked to Coach Barn about you missing archery."

"Oh dear, be easy on her." Her mother attempted a shift towards concern with a nasally delivery. "Alicia, is that bump on your head!?" Her mother exclaimed in shock, letting go of her nose with the intention to console, but quickly drawing herself back, and resuming the same hold once she had moved a good distance from the odor emanating off her daughter.

"Oh my god! It's nothing! I was just with some friends."

"Friends, huh? Real friends would make sure you weren't alone at this hour, they would get you home safe at a reasonable hour!"

"I'm sorry dear, move aside." Her mother interrupted, grabbing hold of Alicia's arm and bringing her into the house. "You are going to wash the river, the dirt and all those god awful smells from your body, clean the tub, and wash up again." Alicia's mother brought her to the foothold of the stairs. "Alicia's washing up now, dear. Is there anything else you want to add?"

"You're grounded! Don't even think of going anywhere or seeing your little friends until I get back from my voyage."

Alicia drudged up the stairs to the bathroom and began washing herself, all the while her parents hurled punishments and empty threats at her. She continued washing even after she was clean. She let the water run through her hair for hours, feeling the droplets travel down her finger and off her palm. Alicia rubbed the bruise on her forehead, the only evidence she had of the day's event. She drained the tub and, using a rag behind the sink, wiped the tub clean. Now her arms and legs were sore, but her bedroom was only a few more steps away. She rinsed the rag one last time, before throwing it behind the sink and heading across the hall. She sighed deeply and threw herself face-first into her sheets. She held tightly to her pillow, screaming deeply into it until she awoke the next morning. Staring at the ceiling one last time, Alicia sprang off her bed and into the bathroom.

"You are not doing this again." Wesley rapped on the bathroom door. "Get out!" Wesley called out, "Mom!" But Alicia stayed to herself in the shower. It gave her peace of mind. She sat down, balled up, and listened to the rushing water. It made her sick, but it also excited her. She hadn't had such a great time since the trip to Apoko fields in 3rd grade, where she and her boyfriend snuck off to the pumpkin patch and held hands, telling each other ghost stories and staring at the clouds.

"That one looks like a giraffe." 9-year-old Alicia squealed. She held onto the boy's hand as they lay looking up at the sky in the old pumpkin patch.

"It looks like a cloud." The boy replied, chuckling.

"No, silly, you've got to imagine, see."

"I still see a cloud," The boy laughed even harder until Alicia hit his arm.

"Ow, what you do that for?" he grabbed her arm.

"Hey, let go of my arm," Alicia whined.

"First, tell me what you did it for," the boy teased.

Alicia looked into his wild eyes, they were vibrant with possibilities. She could never get a read on this boy; maybe that's why she liked him so much. She buried her face in one of the pumpkins. "Alicia! Alicia! Alicia!" he called out, the sound being drowned out by her own brother's pestering.

"Alicia, get out of the damn bath, I need to go!" Wesley put his face to the door so the sound of his voice would disrupt any other sound she could hear or imagine.

"Go outside!" Alicia's face tensed, and she tried to relax under the stream of cool water.

"It's not that type of go!" Wesley snapped back.

"Ughhhh!" Alicia groaned. She stopped the water and put on her towel. Dripping wet, she opened the door to the bathroom, and Wesley rushed in, pants already off, sliding onto the toilet seat. "Really gotta start drying your feet first," he said, covering his eyes with one hand. "This is how dad's boot marks get everywhere," he muttered under his breath.

"Alicia!" Her mother called from below.

"Coming Mom!" Alicia answered with haste. She ran to her room and slammed the door shut behind her, taking her time picking out the day's clothing.

"Alicia!" her mother called once more.

"Coming," she yelled into the hallway. Alicia went into her closet, throwing down a couple of shirts. Rummaging through her dresser, she picked up a few skirts, tossing them on the comforter. As she laid out all the different outfits and possible combinations upon her bed, it occurred to her, she was staying in. There was not much need for pride in her appearance, and her normal pajamas would do for whatever her mother would request.

"Alicia!" her mother called louder, and Alicia met her mother, who half-smirked at her from the bottom of the stairs. "You've got company."

"Company?" Alicia answered, puzzled.

"Go on up, make it quick, her father comes home later tonight, and she isn't supposed to have guests."

"What company are you talking about?"

"Come now, hurry on up," her mother urged.

"Thanks, Mrs. Silverstone,"

"Good to see you again, and thank you. These flowers are lovely, and not even from the front yard this time." Mrs. Silverstone giddily shuffled in place.

The boy tore up the stairs, instantly bumping into Alicia. The two standing face to face on the stairs, just looking into one another's eyes.

"Hey," he said, looking up at her, "I didn't expect you to be so down the stairs."

"Oh God," Alicia looked over to her mom, who went off giggling and excited toward the kitchen. "What is it you want?" Alicia sat down on the finished wooden steps and sighed deeply.

"I'm here to apologize." He uttered breathlessly, holding onto the railing.

Alicia's heart went racing, her eyes widened, and she became more attentive to the situation. The boy, now at face level, with his unkempt fiery hair and doe-eyed innocence, was enough to make her swallow her breath.

"Go on," she managed.

"I don't even know anymore- not like I had anything to do with yesterday. I mean I was there but I think we can all agree I, personally didn't do anything to make you feel that way, so I guess I'm saying-"

"I'm sorry." Laila came charging up the stairs and embraced Alicia, who sat there in awe.

"He said he wanted to apologize first, I just thought-"

"I understand."

"I still don't. I only walked with him because he made it seem-"

"The more frustrated you get, the more he wins."

"That makes absolutely no sense."

"That's Jaden."

"Look, Alicia, you know I'd never do anything to risk our friendship. I'm sorry that I got you into that. I'm sorry I *let that all happen,* just sorry." Laila looked Alicia in the eyes, with an earnestness that slowly overtook her subtle mortification. Alicia accepted her into her arms with force and conviction. The two holding each other wordlessly on the staircase.

"Holy shit! She does have friends." Wesley ran towards the bathroom.

"Make sure you dry your feet, Wesley!" Alicia shouted upstairs.

"It's good that you finally came to the neighborhood. Welcome." Alicia stated plainly before bursting into laughter. The two sat around the table while Alicia's mother brought them sweet macadamia cookies, and they laughed it up while guzzling milk drinks and honey treats. They all had their merriment and enjoyed each other's company. Laila and Alicia mostly harassed a hapless Jaden until he flipped some pudding onto his shirt and adjourned to the other room to freshen up.

"That wasn't nice, Laila." Alicia managed through muffled laughter.

"Honestly, I don't care for him much."

"Me neither, but it scares me when people can hurt the ones who love them like they're collateral damage, and it won't cost them anything." Alicia went quiet for a moment, and Laila flinched.

"It does. It did." Laila swallowed a lump of remorse and regretful impulses. She could feel her head going hot and her breathing becoming hard and rigid as her limbs stiffened with tension. Alicia reached over the table and took Laila's fingers into her palm, brushing the back with her thumb.

"I know." Alicia curled the side of her mouth with a sympathy bordering on pity.

"Alicia, nothing was comfortable. I just wanted to make sure William was safe. I wasn't even sure if I could go through with it, and then Sydney stepped into the blade. I'm positive he did, otherwise I-" Laila made a visor with her fingers covering her head as remorse filled her breathing.

"Laila, you don't have to say anymore. I can feel the pain in your voice, and I know how much you do to protect the people closest to you." Alicia reached out and tenderly grabbed Laila's hand.

"I understand, Alicia. I'm sorry, I need you to know that. For everything. I get it, thanks for being my friend, but I understand if you don't want to hang out anymore." Laila looked sincerely into Alicia's eyes, her lips pressing together with remorse. Alicia burst into laughter, slapping the table and grabbing her stomach as the wind escaped.

"I'm sorry. I'm not laughing at you, just the ridiculousness of what you said. I won't stop hanging out with you because of one bad day." Alicia wiped a tear onto her finger. She leaned over the table, guarding her words from any onlookers.

"I don't think I could ever stop hanging out with you. You're my best friend, Laila. I care about you more than anyone. Ever since I've known you, you've been Laila. Even the days I want to scream at you, it's just you being too you and sometimes that person is the only one I wanna just sit back with and talk about the day with, thanks for allowing me to cherish all that, even if I don't care too much about your other friends." Alicia fiddled with her thumbs, before looking up at Laila with a small grin.

"You know who I really don't care for?" Laila moved closer to Alicia by sliding her palm across the table.

"Who?"

"Chesney Adams," she said, her eyebrows raising with a hesitant look.

"His breath stinks," said Alicia, breaking the silence. Their chatter evolved into uproarious laughter. Suddenly, Jaden came tumbling down the stairs with a series of thuds and stuttered groans.

"Wet steps." He got up, rubbing a tender spot on the top of his head. He looked at Alicia and Laila and smiled. They gathered their things and went off towards the door. The roar of thunder sent Alicia crashing to the floor. "Oh no, kids, you can't go home in this weather," Mrs. Silverstone's voice came rushing in from the parlor.

The kids stared back blank and expressionless.

"Thanks, Mrs. Silverstone, but it wouldn't be home if there were clear skies."Laila blandly muttered.

"Nonsense! This will lighten up in a moment. I couldn't look your father in the eyes at my next physical if I let you go out in this." Mrs. Silverstone guided her towards the living room.

"Personally, I think he'd prefer that." Laila's eyes darted around the room. It was a quaint living space, despite her trips to the bathroom, she hadn't really looked around too much. She knew that Alicia had a lot of extracurriculars, but it was something about the pride with which her mother displayed those abandoned pursuits that warmed Laila's heart with a similar admiration. There was a crudely done self-portrait from her artistry years. A short poem pinned to the picture. Directly across from the poem was Alicia's archery bow. Under the bow were her tap shoes.

"Alicia, why don't you play that violin your father got you?"

"It's a viola, Mom." Alicia went over to the coffee table in the middle of the painting and bow, and opened a case resting atop. The viola was crafted with a very light wood, so it appeared almost ivory when it shone in a particular lighting. The streaks going across the body were very small but gave a clear indication of what the instrument was carved from. The F-holes almost shone in the way that they captured the light. Keeping just dim enough for the jet-black fingerboard to leave each string visible.

"You know Alicia's father got her that all the way from the oxent. It blocks light so well, it's the only thing she can play with no glasses." Mrs. Silverstone sat on a faded, worn blue chair.

"They don't wanna hear about the Occident," Alicia whined.

"Oh, I very much think they do," Mrs. Silverstone crossed her legs and patted her blue gingham gown. "See, Alicia had just started band practice and told her father-"

"Mom, I'm playing. I need quiet when I start." Alicia tapped the rosin on the table. She picked up the viola first, seating it neatly under her chin. Her fingers automatically shifted into a claw, and each stood completely still above the strings. In another swift motion, she picked up the bow and began to brush it against one of the chords. The room was deathly silent as the melody rang out. Laila and Jaden sat on the couch, feeling an overwhelming sense of Deja Vu. Their bodies had almost a rigid and tense feeling from the rhythm. Jaden's face lit up with recognition, and he began humming along.

"The prestige and wisdom, our elite academy," Laila's voice joined the hum. She began singing in a tone a little lower than Jaden's humming. Alicia picked up on their recall and smiled as she continued to churn out the tune that they hesitantly remembered. They didn't vocalize now, they just let the music overtake the room as Mrs. Silverstone brimmed with pride.

"It's the school anthem!" Alicia stopped playing to announce.

"Alicia! There's one more flourish." Mrs. Silverstone raised. Laila and Jaden began clapping, as embarrassing and shameful as it was to applaud any pride related to Prestige Academy, they knew that their solidarity would overwrite her mother's criticism.

"It's the only one I know by heart." Alicia laughed, took a deep breath and hugged both of their necks so tightly they may have lost balance if they weren't already seated. The rain had begun to lighten up, and the streams going down the window shortly turned to droplets careening down the surface. Mrs. Silverstone protested heavily, and Alicia silently agreed with her mother, but after some small pushback and the mention of the rain getting worse, they were able to make their way out of the manor. Mrs. Silverstone had fitted them with shawls and oversized hats that would undoubtedly become soaked as the moisture accumulated in the material. Still, they left with the items propped on their person, sacrificing their mobility in an attempt to alleviate some of the woman's worry.

— CHAPTER 11 —

"So pneumonia?" William asked. It wasn't the first time he had been home since the fire, but it had been so long that much dust had accumulated. His stomach hadn't been settling well after his last meal, and after much protest, Laila had decided to walk with him back to his house. It wasn't a long walk, seeing as they were not far from the old schoolyard, but still, it helped his belly deflate a little more to where the swelling had almost gone down entirely. The roads were just as scorched as the surrounding buildings, and the ash stuck to their feet as they made their way across the charred, barren landscape. There were no creatures stirring about, nor insects buzzing in the air. The fire had truly decimated the land, and whoever burned this village ensured that not even the dirt would be safe from cauterization. Nothing could grow, and the land was no longer arable. It's only fitting that time refused to move forward from the day of the fire in William's old house. They had long taken down the Swing set that hung outside his window. He had no idea which member of the village had completed the act, only that they forgot to take down the entire building, or maybe they had grown weary with the tragedy, and the most their capacity would allow would be a simple taking down of a regular swing set. The floor had holes down to the foundation where the scorched earth was visible in some parts, and the entire first floor had been charred to an unrecognizable state. The stairs had patches of black ash, and as they ascended the stairs, their footprints were left behind like fresh steps in the snow. William swore everything was fine and agreed going to Alicia's house to apologize was a good idea, and he would need some time to clean up after his nap, either way. He took a blanket from the closet, shook it off and laid it on his bed. Laila offered to bring him some snacks, but his stomach hadn't fully gone down, and although he didn't verbally reject the offer, he did crawl into bed and doze off until he awoke to the sound of a hacking cough.

"Yea didn't think it'd be that bad. I had a really good time until you know," Jaden said, kicking a heap of clothes to the side.

"And what about-"

"She's fine, I walked her home." Jaden rummaged through a pile of clothing in the closet until his arm went through a wall.

"Wait, you actually walked her home this time?" William sat himself up on the bed.

"Yea." Jaden shook some dust off his arm before wiping it on a nearby uniform shirt.

"What'd Doc say?" William asked, staring off at the droplets lining up across his charred window pane.

"Ah, you know it's really bad, thinks I only have about six days to get my affairs in order," Jaden stopped himself in the middle of sleeving his arm.

William shot an accusatory glance.

"Okay, it's six months, but no one can really predict an exact timeline with cases of terminal boredom." Jaden chuckled at his own joke, then looked at William, who sat stone-faced.

"What did her parents say Jaden?" William specified.

"I left when we got to her door," Jaden replied, sleeving the other arm.

"Well, now I can't get back to bed." William rose up.

"Yeah, I wouldn't go out there," Jaden answered, buttoning his shirt.

"You need to quit this homeless drifter thing you've been doing. Do you even know where you died?"

"Somewhere along a sandy beach and a starry coastline," Jaden answered. He threw on a pair of William's uniform shorts, which looked like boxers in comparison to the length of Jaden's legs. He walked over to the window to watch the rain droplets as they gathered the luminescence of the stars as best as they were able to on the black, scorched glass. He looked over at all the leveled buildings, immured and broken. He watched across the way at the platform of wood charred to a shade less visible than the night.

"What about you? Preaching all this changing up routine, and now you're literally living in the ashes of your past. Doesn't this give you tingles? All that's happened here, that's why you can't sleep. Why don't you try to move back in with Walter? Or stay with Ephriam? Or-"

"Don't you dare suggest that," William retorted sharply.

"The doctor." Jaden finished. William looked away. He didn't have the words to explain how staying under the Doctor's roof felt too much like defeat and, more importantly, a reminder of every failure in his efforts and character.

"I just can't, alright, I have a goal and-" William's eyes scanned the room, trying to find a spot that didn't remind him of his tragedy.

"Yeah, I get it, do what you have to do, man. I'll help you fix this place up after your goal." Jaden yawned and stretched until the long-sleeved uniform shirt revealed his forearm.

"Deal." They both said in unison.

"You know where I'll be," Jaden sat on the floor, and they laughed. The tension had completely cleared, and they both laid back.

"I can't believe it's already been 3 years," Jaden crossed his left leg atop his right.

"That's because every day feels like it happened yesterday." William put his face in his palms.

"You keep living every day like it's yesterday, may as well have just left me on the ground, dude."

"I know man, and I know I haven't been myself. It feels like I'm playing catch-up, trying to get back to me, so I can live in the present. I think in the fall, maybe after my birthd-"

"Hey, remember back when we first met?" Jaden mentioned abruptly.

"You mean when we were lined up for the fire drill and you pushed everyone down the stairs and blamed me even though I was in front?" William sighed.

"Nah, a little further than that, the day after school, our first adventure."

"The one where the dessert shop turned out to be run by cannibals?"

"Nah man, even before that, the first day we met each other."

"Oh, you mean that time when you were with your dad!"

"Exactly!" Jaden replied, snapping, so his finger pointed towards William.

"I wasn't going to do anything; I was just going to let my dad get shot right in front of me. Not like I wanted to, but I felt like I couldn't move, even if the gun wasn't pointed at me, I thought that the gun decided my fate. It wasn't until you swept that dude's leg and he fell into my fist, that I realized I'm kicking this guy's ass, whether I'm ready or not, but win or lose, this kid's my best friend. Now a dude-face-shaped heartbreak just fell on your fist, what are you going to do now?"

— CHAPTER 12 —

Alicia tapped her desk impatiently. She had to keep herself not only composed but quiet enough that she would not incur the ire of the chatty educator.

"I'm not here to tell you the answer, I'm here to teach you," Ephriam droned on and on about the general subject of education, much to everyone's discontent. That was the fifth time he made that exact same statement. Alicia sat, patting her desk impatiently. Much like the majority of the class, she had grown accustomed to the instructor's deviation from the lesson. Cadence and Guilliam were absent, leaving a sort of vacuum in the front of the class. Bryce and Venna sat on opposite ends in the front row, attentively taking notes on Ephriam's rant. Saphron showed up late. She had been arriving late to class for a while now that she separated from the people who had actively motivated and crafted her punctuality. The green-eyed girl didn't even turn once to her classmates, just drudging down to her row, diving straight into her book.

"Poor Saphron," Alicia murmured, not just for the girl who had drifted away from the group but also for the loneliness and longing she recognized all too well in her classmate's movements. Laila gazed longingly out the window as usual. She hadn't picked up on the tension of the classroom, but she rarely voluntarily involved herself in classroom discourse. Times like these, Alicia wished she could express such matters to her former bandmate, Tran Aimee. The bandmates that Alicia had hung out with remained cordial, but they were more acquaintances who waved to each other and wrote notes on special occasions. Alicia patted Saphron's desk even more impatiently, before letting out a long, "Psttt," to Saphron.

"Young lady, we do not pst in the middle of a lesson," Ephriam chided.

"Got it. No pst when you start teaching... Pssstttt," Alicia went to Saphron.

"Young lady!" Ephriam sang, his voice getting shrill.

"Psttttt '' Alicia and Ephriam gestured simultaneously.

"Wake up, Saphron!" The old, balding teacher bellowed.

"Huh? I wasn't sleeping." Saphron turned with a page of the book still stuck to her cheek, the rest of the class laughing at her absurd predicament.

"She probably couldn't sleep, poor thing spent the night pining over the love of her life." Frannesca snickered.

"Hiding her devastation with a book," Dayvonna shook her head. Using her compact mirror to make eye contact with Sieya.

"Does anyone have any gum?" Chesney Adams asked. They all made their own jokes and theories about her lack of sleep, and it took Ephriam a while to calm the clamor of the room.

"I will leave this nursery house of a school again! Keep trying me!"

"When are you even here?" Venna maintained eye contact with the hulking educator.

"I know this is the only class left, but I still want to request a transfer," Frannesca added.

While his attention was redirected, Alicia made another attempt. "Psstt,"

"What! What is so important you keep pestering me?!" Saphron said loud enough into the crook of her elbow.

"We're all hanging out after school, you should come along. I'll wait for you, and we can ditch practice together." Alicia tapped the seat of her chair. "This is probably the first time you talked to me all school year." Saphron moved the leg of the chair further from Alicia's hand.

"Well, better late than never, right? Besides, my glasses broke, and I can't really practice without them." Alicia cheekily smiled.

"Ephriam's speaking. I need to take notes."

"Okay, but if you change your mind, we can try to wait until after practice before we all hang out. Right, Laila?" Alicia turned to see the window hanging open and Laila missing from her seat. She turned to the front of the room and patted her desk impatiently.

"Drellavitz, you need to put the mirror away, I said away- I don't care if it's Dayvonna's, she can get it from you after class. Now put it away!" Ephriam chided. Sieya Drellavitz's eyes narrowed in her compact mirror, and she closed it and put it in her bag. Kicking the bag to Dayvonna Marsai once the ends were closed. Ephriam continued to reprimand his students as he walked back down the aisle to his desk, which resembled a toy when positioned next to his form.

"You kids have had all weekend to play disharmonious music, instruments away!" Ephriam barked, posturing himself as a disapproving conductor, as he leaned forward, looking over two or three aisles to address the kids, who shuffled their bows and reeds begrudgingly like an orchestra forced into silence mid-overture. Tran Aimee closed her cello case, and Lofley Crishen placed his drumsticks flat in a groove that was dug in at the ends of all their desks. Presumably, so the floor wouldn't need to be leveled, and pens, along with other writing instruments, could situate themselves atop without rolling or dropping from the surface. Otto Vancleve lowered his woodwind instrument, keeping the reed entirely out of sight.

"I have eyes in the back of my head, and they're always watching... Like a hawk!" Ephriam walked back to the front of the classroom.

"Now, class, turn your textbook to page- Saphron! You need to pay attention, you were already late, and then asleep! You need to catch up to the rest of the lecture like your peers." Ephriam singled out Saphron, putting his focus on the girl, who rested her head upon her hand wearily, as the entire classroom stirred.

"Yes yes the seventh lecture about teaching," Alicia murmured to herself.

"Huh?" Saphron replied, the comment Alicia had thrown her off, and Ephriam naturally added to frustration.

"Look, we skipped you ahead, but maybe that was a bit of a rushed judgment."

"Jeez, she's just tired. It's not that serious, Ephriam," Kerwin stared up at the man. Then the ceiling as Ephriam stiffened his leg and in an instant his foot rose up and kicked Kerwin's only pencil out of the boy's hand, and straight up to the lead-dotted ceiling.

"I wasn't asleep!" Saphron defended.

"Why you gotta do that to people children?" Susanna's inflections peaked on certain words, giving her voice a melodic tone. Susanna, like Kerwin, Anthony and Kerrigan, was a generational native and, as a result, had internalized much of the island's culture. This included mannerisms, attitudes, and dialects of the surrounding areas. Anthony and Kerrigan sucked their teeth in accordance with her outburst.

"I would have just stabbed him with the pencil." Venna looked into Ephriam's eyes as she said the phrase. Venna was much like the majority of the island's population, first generation. Her family had moved from their home in the Occident, not long before she was born.

"I have permission from his grandmother and great-grandfather." Ephriam plucked the pencil from the ceiling.

"Our great-grandfather died before we were born. What the hell are you talking about?" Anthony answered for Kerwin.

"A promise I intend to keep." Ephriam took a deep breath. "Now I can't very well ensure your or these young men's survival if you sleep through my course."

"I wasn't asleep! I just daydreamed a little!" Saphron said as she tried to hide a yawn.

"Well, thanks to Saphron's dream, the rest of you can spend an extra hour in school today," Ephriam announced proudly. It only takes one infraction to lead to total chaos. He had successfully maintained the harmony of his classroom, and no doubt would be covertly adjusted by those with similar desires to learn and equal passions for education.

" Don't blame her. It's not Saphon's fault you let every rolling cloud take away from the lesson." Alicia clarified, smiling at Saphron briefly, before returning to her defiant staredown. Saphron stared wide-eyed and frozen, reticently shaking her head with disapproval.

"The clown leaves, and of course, it's Silverstone who decides to take up the bauble." Ephriam slowly clapped as he sat atop his desk.

"And just because you have nothing better to do than obsess over students who know you aren't worth their time doesn't mean you can take up our… Time!" Alicia said, looking up at the man. The entire class applauded her bravery, whistling in agreement, even Otto churned out a celebratory pitch on his woodwind.

"Head master's office. Now!" Ephriam pointed Alicia out the door. The class now changed their tone to ooohs, chuckles and other instigative sounds that accompanied her disruption. Alicia walked through the aisle past her chuckling classmates. She only lamented that soon after she left the door of the classroom that Ephriam would be directly behind her, providing a comprehensive reflection of her actions.

"The reason I teach is to keep you kids out of trouble. There are too many dangers on this island to prepare you for, and I'm doing my best to prepare you all for not only the island but the world."

"Does kicking your ass mean we're prepared enough?" Alicia said without looking back at the man's expression.

"Oh, you think you're funny, you think that's funny, there's much more to life than fighting, and that is the message I'm trying to impart as you kids reach your final days of academia. That village was burnt in ignorance, not aggression. There is a way we do things on *this island* because of *who* comes to this island. Sure, some students may have the tools to quote "kick *my ass*" unquote, but to call yourself a student of Ephriam; That's an honor only a few gain, but it is a title that is observed without being addressed." Ephriam spoke confidently and held his nose up with an almost condescension.

"What are you talking about?" Alicia stopped in her tracks and turned around to share her expression of confusion and bewilderment.

"We'll speak more when we reach the headmaster's office," Ephriam said solemnly.

"Why? What's even the point of going all this way? No one can hear us over here, and it's your office!" Alicia raised her voice slowly until she was essentially screaming down the hall, with the full knowledge that whether her classmates overheard her or not, they wouldn't peer into the hallway.

"There's a world beyond this island. That world won't be as kind to you as this island." Ephriam spoke slowly and solemnly.

"Which part of this island is kind?" Alicia took a deep breath and closed her eyes in frustration.

"Sure, it may seem dangerous, but a cruel person does not compare to a cruel system. It's what I try to tell you all. There are so many ways to be corrupted and deluded by this world. This is why I've been educating not just your class, but generations of this island's population. You need to have the knowledge to see through their false accounts, the resilience to withstand their extreme prejudices and the wherewithal to challenge the wicked intentions of others. Equipped with only your courage, integrity and just a bit of luck at your side. Please tell me you've read at least the first page of your textbook." Ephriam genuinely pleaded, the softness of his eyes being obscured slightly by a glare from his glasses, leaving his expression entirely out of Alicia's field of vision.

"Why don't you just teach the textbook?" Alicia's frustration morphed into a penitent expression as her brow relaxed.

"That's all I'm ever trying to do! I usually don't have this many students by now, and you kids can be a lot to manage! You know, the previous generations understood the importance of education; they didn't have some wannabe Lancelot to come to their rescue in their time of need. The only thing to come to their aid was the skills and knowledge myself and Prestige Academy imparted for their survival."

Ephriam's eyes softened into pools of emotion that basted his look with a quiet sadness.

"Ephriam, I'm not gonna feel sorry for you that we didn't die." Alicia's voice grew louder, and her brow furrowed as her confusion was once more replaced by frustration.

"Not every battle can be solved by fighting, and not every problem can be thought through. Let's continue on to the headmaster's office." Ephriam sighed.

"Ephriam, I'm about two seconds from leaving out the same window as Laila." Alicia crossed her arms and tapped her foot impatiently.

"Wait, where's Laila?"

—— CHAPTER 13 ——

"So all I'm saying is we go for one easier to defeat first, you know, like pecking order." Jaden threw in.

"You're literally the only one that died last time." William raised his head from the pillow.

"Look, let's just go for something a little easier, like look right there, chicken." Jaden pointed to the page. They had spent the hours of the night and into the morning combing through the books that were left in a chest in William's parents' room. The room had several holes in the floor, and a large portion of the ceiling had been rained in, but somehow, with all the pouring rain and collapsing lumber, the chest survived. William found himself taking count of all the scars on the wall that gave his chest a burning similar to what the property endured. The searing sensation only grew more intense as William approached the chest he had seen throughout his childhood, but never had gone through the contents until now. Being in the wreckage of his old parents' room brought him back to days of adventures where he'd come home, eat dinner, collapse in his bed and barely spend time at home, much less his parents' room. Whenever he found himself in that room, it wasn't to ask about the chest. He actually found the item mundane, almost blending into the scenery. Now the fire-scorched walls and gaps in the ash-laden flooring made the object stand out as the only item reminiscent of his carefree years. Jaden put a reconciling hand on his shoulder and soothed his back. William hesitated and swallowed deep as he prepared to unshroud more grief he tried to ignore.

"We don't have to do this now, we can wait until you're ready. This can still happen tomorrow or even next week-or right now, right now also works." Jaden patted the air as William dove into the chest mid-sentence. It was at the very bottom that they saw the book, etched with carvings of different animals all going around a circle as if they were chasing after or succeeding one another.

"Rooster." William corrected. "Yeah, looks easy enough. Honestly, I don't even know which ones are which."

"Huh?" Jaden questioned.

"With Sydney, it was different. I had a gut feeling."

"Gut feeling?"

"Yeah, like hunger. The closer I got to him, the hungrier I got. It's weird, I took a walk the other day, and even now I can still feel that hunger." William pressed in the area around his stomach, still feeling a phantom distention, despite not having eaten since his previous meal.

"So, how do you feel now?" Jaden closed the book and gave William his full attention.

"I could eat," William retorted, poking down the folds of his shirt.

"Think chicken." Jaden laughed.

Suddenly, there came a knocking sound from downstairs.

"William!" Laila called out, "I'm coming in!" A moment later, Laila sprang up the charred steps to William's room. The door being left slightly cracked open put emphasis on the sound of her feet beating against the broken wood. The beats grew closer together as she arrived at the top.

"Was school good?" Jaden jeered. She ignored the comment and jumped at William, who sat in bed. She could feel her shame welling up from the proximity and her heart nearly jumping from her chest. She powered through the feeling and slowly lowered her head onto his shoulder. It was something about his calmness, or maybe the comfortability that brought her a slowness her racing mind rarely experienced. She looked up at him, but he stared off into the distance without so much as a tense in the shoulder or sweat on the forehead. It was a little liberating, and it did make things much easier. Laila wrapped her arms around William's neck and pecked his cheek before jumping back, planting her feet on the floor. Since the incident, she had tried to restore his identity, and showing affection at this point was almost second-nature. This, however, would only be the second time she kissed him. The first time happened a little after she got moved up to their class. A good amount of time before the fire. The teasing had been so relentless for both of them, neither could talk to their families about the harassment. This could have been the reason Jaden blurted out their business, which anyone with eyes could notice. It could have also easily been to distract from his own indiscretions. Either way, it escalated the conflict. It was only in the secrecy of the forest that they were able to speak without expectation or observation, she replied to his frustrations. "If you haven't lost at anything so far, maybe you should keep at it, you know, for the record?"

"Good Morning!" she cawed out and waved awkwardly.

"Good Morning," William responded plainly.

"So we've decided to kill the chicken next," Jaden threw in to interrupt the tension or lack thereof.

"Does it work like that?" Laila questioned, dusting herself off and standing nearer to the bedside.

"It doesn't." William sighed.

"Wait, that chest? I've never seen that chest before… No way! Is that Sandra's?" Laila dove next to the chest and took stock of the item on the floor. She sat on her knees and felt the ridges of the wood. There were many patterns that seemed to be designed through metalwork. Either side of the chest had this intricate metalwork running the length in two strips. The design around the lock, and what may have clued Laila into the true nature of this chest, was the N, W, S, and E around the slot where the key would be inserted. It would give the lock the appearance of a compass. Laila opened the lid and began rummaging through the contents. There were mostly maps, but they all seemed to be from different time periods. Laila could see the similarities in some of the maps, but there was greater differentiation in the sizing and position of certain areas and borders. She searched further, and she saw a few books that seemed to be filled with recipes and other gardening tips. After picking a few up, she nearly dropped them all back into the chest, upon noticing a book with a similar symbol to the one inscribed on the chest. She placed the book all to one side and picked it up excitedly. She opened it to the first page, and it was blank. She put her head closer to the book, not ruling out that the font could be incredibly faded or small. She continued to flip through the pages, and William moved himself to the edge of the bed. She flipped to the end and, rather than flip to the last page, she held the book upside down, and a small folded paper flitted past her fingers before she snatched it out of the air, dropping the book an inch or two away from the toe of her shoe.

"Yes! Yes! I knew it!" Laila unfolded the paper excitedly.

"Laila, you just got here, but I'm the one who found the important book." Jaden held up the book with the animal inscriptions.

"Laila, what is it?" William sat up on the edge.

"She did it! She drew a map of the world! I'm sure it needs a little fact-checking- I mean, William, how often did you see your mom leave the island?" Laila stretched the map, adjusting her fingers, due to the length of the paper being far greater than her tiny frame. She spread it out neatly on the opening of the chest.

"Never. She has never left since I was born." William stood over Laila, looking down at the girl as she smoothed the edges of the map.

"Exactly, since you were born. Just like my mom, your parents came to this island from somewhere else. Sandra never told you about the sailors? The ones she'd take on tours? Who'd tell her stories about the New World?" Laila turned around, growing more frustrated by the moment with the absence of a response.

"Again. Never." William tried to abate the tension.

"Well, all you have to know is this is one of the few maps in the world that covers the Occident, Orient, and the New World! We can get anywhere in the world with this!" Laila waved her hand through the air, like a chef presenting a fresh meal.

"It is impressive, especially since she's never been off the island." Jaden cocked his head to the side.

"Right there, that little spot in the middle, that's our island! So, which part of the map makes you hungry?" Laila hovered her finger just above the map, waiting for William to give her an indication.

"Also, not how it works," William added.

"I could have told you that," Jaden sang over her head. She turned around sharply.

"No, he couldn't." William placed a hand on her shoulder, gently reassuring her.

"So, where to now?" Laila began folding the map along the creases.

"The South West coast." William stated, "I'm getting a vibe from there."

CHAPTER 14

The shoreline stretched in every direction, the breeze picked up the rolling waves as their plumes washed ashore, dissolving the sand into more of the ocean. The entire area was teeming with movement but devoid of any life. The next town must have been only a couple hours by land, and that same thought lit their minds abuzz. How long would it take to get to the nearest town by sea? What would that place be like? What possibilities could this new land hold?

"Nothing, there's nothing here at all," Jaden angrily kicked the sand. "It'd be nice if you two would help." Laila and William stared out over the horizon at the waves that came crashing in. He took her hand into his and held it gently. The gesture did not have the intended effect of reassurance or consideration. Laila threw his hand towards the ground and jumped away, before taking a deep breath and coming closer to William's side.

"They're not all on the island, are they?" Alicia plopped herself in the sand and let go of a large sigh.

"It would seem that way," William responded, eyes still glued to the horizon.

"There's a huge landmass that way, according to the map. It shouldn't be more than a day to get there." Laila looked up at where William stared and adjusted herself until she found the place on the map closest to his gaze.

"So what do we do?" Alicia questioned once more.

"We get a boat," William answered.

"Okay, what about those pirates that y'know we?" Jaden began.

"That's actually not a half-bad idea. You think there was a ship by?" William cut Jaden off as he mimicked loading a shotgun.

"You all really love poking the bear, don't you?" Laila rushed in before William could finish his thought.

"It's funny you say that," Jaden finished cocking his imaginary shotgun.

"It's genuinely not the same thing, and what the hell are you doing?" William raised at Jaden.

"I know, right? I can't even think with this-whatever he's doing." Laila groaned.

"Well, to be fair, Walter did catch the first one." Jaden mimicked slicing his own neck.

"Look, we don't need to ask Walter, we'll just check if the ship's nearby," William said,

"How many pirates dock on this part of the island? I didn't see any ship that morning." Laila folded her arms.

"I'm following literally zero of what's going on right now." Alicia looked at everyone's expression for answers. "I'm going to need to be informed of decisions from now on for this team-up to work. Laila, I'm two seconds-"

"It's an old friend of ours, he owns a bar and a little fishing vessel." Laila interrupted.

"A bar? None of you are old enough to go to a bar, Laila, you're like twelve."

"Wow, really, Alicia? My birthday's in like a few months. I'm basically thirteen."

"Still sounds like twelve in my book." Jaden reached for her face, and Laila snapped at his hand.

"He can't come." Laila pointed her finger at Jaden, who was holding his finger protectively.

"That's fine, I was planning on buying a ship for whenever William's done staring down the barrel of Walter's gun." Jaden turned away from the provocation.

"Yeah, so I never thought I'd say this again, but I'm going with Jaden." Alicia nearly gagged at the thought.

"Sounds fine to me," William waved.

"Love how much you're learning from this Walter guy," Alicia raised her eyebrows.

William turned around, and Laila palmed her face.

"What's that supposed to mean?" William's face was completely devoid of any expression, and the words seemed like whispers.

"I'm saying this isn't the William I know. The William I know wouldn't-"

"Alicia, things happened to me, I know you saw it, there's a person I have to be now. I don't want to do these things, but look where the loose ends got us."

"You can't be shouldering the weight of that fire; you were a kid. You're still a kid!" Alicia raised her hand to fix her glasses, but pulled her hand back to her side.

"That's the exact problem, that naivety that led me to bring strangers into our village, looking for a treasure I had no concept of beforehand, now that treasure haunts me every day, I can't keep believing I can be better than what I've been made. I've seen where it goes." William looked Alicia in the eyes with a cold, impassive stare.

"That problem was why we became friends in the first place, it's why Jaden calls you his best friend and why Laila-"

"This is why I didn't want this starting in the first place, my name doesn't need to be associated anytime William is brought up. We're our own people." Laila cringed at her own sentiment. She had spent enough time making similar statements, but now the words felt bitter, and filled her throat with mucus. "I mean-"

"It does help cushion the blow," Jaden added, placing a consoling hand upon her shoulder. "And this one might need bulletproof padding."

— CHAPTER 15 —

William brought himself over to the bar door. He couldn't see anything that was going on inside, only the clamor of various pots and pans, as well as muffled words, and various footfalls and stomps. It was hard to interpret anything going on in the room, and William found it eased his mind the wood was already falling out of polish. Before long it would lose even more character, if it didn't need to be outright replaced. He stood there, feeling the cold seabreeze tingle his limbs, unsure of whether to warm himself with his hands, or find somewhere the wind couldn't reach. Nearly shivering as he stood inches away from another home that called to his belonging, until it required his abandonment. He loathed the idea of asking his former guardian for more favors, especially now that he found himself distanced from the stewardship. William could remember after the fire, he could fit all his things into the bag. He stood looking at the old tavern wall, and the sheen that came from the rain that grew moss underneath. There was no turning back now. Walter had been kind enough to offer him work after the funeral, but it was much easier and admittedly more comfortable to sleep in the quarters of the ship, or clear a space in the tavern, than to rest in the ashes of his past. The aging barkeep had actually preferred he stay until he preferred him to leave. Now here he was asking the man for more kindness. No matter how he wished things were different or dreamt up other possibilities, he slowly came to the realization. This is yet another matter out of my control. The moments passed slower than ever. Standing on those tavern steps, unsure if he could draw closer but unable to shake the temptation of returning to ease and comfort.

"Like hell!" He heard Walter's sonorous tone and cringed. The rushed, definite footsteps filled his ears before the door flew back, leaving him and Walter standing almost face to face.

"The sea is a dangerous place, William!" Walter chucked a bag of William's things at him.

"Yeah, you keep saying that, but this island really isn't any better." William caught the bag and looked up at Walter.

"You have no idea what's out there!" He bellowed into the generous space between the last step that separated the two.

"Can't be that much worse than what's out here..." Just then, William saw the little brunette poking her head out, she attempted to creep past Walter.

"And you!" Laila felt a shock go through her spine that halted all movement, even the thought.

Walter grabbed hold of her cheeks and pulled them in two different directions, almost lifting her off the ground.

"What would you ever need my old fishing vessel for? Second thought, don't answer that. Just get to school, I'm sure Ephriam would be delighted to see the two of you." Walter nudged Laila out of the doorway and slammed the door on William's foot.

"I'm not giving you-"

"Thanks for everything, Walter." Just then, Walter saw the boy he had raised transformed into a man before his very eyes. He had never heard, much less seen, such a deep, passionate look in his ward's eyes. He grinned slightly. Kicked William's foot and slammed the door shut. "Ow!"Laila complained, rubbing her cheeks.

"I'm sorry." William opened

"Don't be, that was actually kind've cool." She attempted to smile but recoiled from the soreness in her face. She kicked his shin in frustration and stormed down the steps, while William hopped, grabbing the affected area. He couldn't help his eyes being drawn to the vessel; it seemed so far out of his reach, despite it being a tangible item to grasp. The boat floated at the edge of the dock, and William began to wonder about the care with which the ship was maintained, and whether or not he could restore a boat even to the dilapidated level it had reached. He knew how to steer a boat and had done so on many occasions, but he still had trouble with rough water, although that was more a fault of the stiff rudder than his steering. He'd have much less trouble with a new boat and wouldn't need to repair as much, but Walter had never once bridged the topic of a new ship while repairing the damages to his vessel.

"How much?" Jaden asked the merchant. The only shipyard on the island had to be placed inside, due to the frequent rains and torrential downpours. It was hardly a shipyard and more of a boating shop holding dinghies, kayaks, and canoes. The larger boats were on the ground, and a few of the lighter ones hung overhead in odd corners of the store.

The shopkeeper responded, put on glasses, and leaned over the creaky wooden chair before examining the price tag.

"A lot.

"Can I pay you in labor and housekeeping?" Jaden rolled up his sleeves and hocked a loogie into his palm before smashing it together and rubbing the coating on his skin. He put out his hand.

"Absolutely not." The shopkeep lowered his glasses and glared at Jaden until he put his hand away.

"Well, that's kind've my usual form of payment without William." Jaden shrugged his shoulders.

"Why'd we even come here if you have no money?" Alicia asked with a deep sigh and exasperated eyes that were nearly closed as she bayed her sea of frustrations.

"You can still go places if you don't have money; you just need someone else's money. How much do you got, Alicia?" Jaden tapped the top of his head. Alicia's agitation grew, and reflexively, she smacked Jaden across the arm.

"Oh, right, that could get really twisted. *Do you have enough money for-*" Jaden spoke slowly and to an almost condescending level until Alicia's face soured to the point of interrupting his prior thought.

"We're leaving." She grabbed Jaden's arm and led him out of the store.

"I'm not rich." Alicia pointed out that they were a few feet away from the store's entrance.

"Alicia, I've been to your house. Why don't rich people ever want to just help?" Jaden whined.

"We're not rich, Jaden! My dad just-?" Alicia stopped herself mid-sentence as a realization crept across her mind. She walked away from Jaden, and a deep contemplation formed as she placed her fist under her chin.

"Yes?" Jaden responded, breaking the silence along with a lone breeze.

"What about my village?" Alicia turned back towards Jaden.

"What about it?"

"Come." She took hold of his wrist and dragged him away once more.

Night came and went, the morning sprinkled dewdrops across the grass, and the cicadas hummed gently. A passing crow dove into the field and sat passively. It cawed before reaching its beak into the soft earth to find nutrients. The insects scattered across the field, being picked one by one by the small crow. A worm peered out at the beak and crawled further into the hole, hoping the bird would be satisfied with what it had been ingesting. The bird continued munching and raising its beak to swallow crickets, beetles, and other tasty morsels before diving even deeper into the hole it created. The worm shimmied desperately down the passage as it watched its home, empty of all the creatures that would now assist in its survival. As it seemed the great jaws would devour it whole, the bird flew off, and the worm, not aware, crawled ever deeper into the hole searching for sanctuary. Over that hole is where Jaden laid the pictures down.

"Look, they all fetch a fair price."

"I like it, but I'm surprised you came up with this," Laila interjected.

"I didn't. I swiped a couple of posters from my dad's desk; he won't miss them." Alicia grinded her teeth nervously.

"They could prove difficult to locate," William said, rising from the ground.

"Right there." Laila pointed to a picture of a bearded pirate, "Isn't that the captain Walter got? All we need to do is ask him where he hid the body. I mean it's not much, but it's something to start-"

"No," William stated dryly. He picked the picture up and tore it in half.

"Let's not waste any more time than we need to, Alicia. Which of these guys fetches the highest bounty?"

"Are you sure?" Alicia asked hesitantly. She took one look at William, reached into her bag and pulled out another slip of paper. Jaden took one look at it and smiled, Laila raised her eyebrows, and William studied the image carefully.

"Wow. This guy is more than those two combined." William looked at the paper, awestruck.

"All three of them belonged to the same ravenous gang that terrorized nations, freed prisoners and even facilitated coups to overthrow governments." Alicia brought her fingers up and then slammed them on her side as she realized she couldn't fix her glasses.

"Maybe we should just dig up the pirate corpse." Laila offered, stepping away from the group and rubbing her temples.

"I think we can beat them." Jaden clenched his fist with confidence.

"What do you mean, beat them? This isn't a game," Alicia sneered. "These guys are international criminals. Do you even know what chance there is at finding men like this around here?"

"She's right." William stated, "So we better get looking."

—— CHAPTER 16 ——

"You should really turn back," William glanced back with a side-eye.

"So you'd rather have Jaden at your side?" Laila smiled sardonically while nodding her head slowly.

"Laila, that's not what I'm saying, and you know it."

"No, I get it, you don't have to worry about him dying, but you don't have to worry about me getting hurt." She tilted her head with the same sarcastic grin.

"I'm gonna worry if I can't even guarantee my own safety." William fully stopped and turned towards the girl.

"Then maybe you should be the one turning back." Laila cheekily smirked, patting his back as she took the lead.

"Laila, they may be right about this one. My dad probably collects more bounties than anyone on the island, and he's never even spoken about this place once." Alicia shivered, and her eyes scrolled across the smoking scenery.

"Alicia, I'm going." Laila walked off, William quickly matched her strides, and they went off into the "town". Monarch Cove wasn't a town; it was more of a lawless settlement, with the harbor at the coast, many sailors had taken up residence in the shanty buildings that lined this faux hamlet. They built all of it themselves. Such houses that came and went as the sailors did. A thick smog covered everything from the bay to the wooded dwelling. The earth was scorched and devoid of life, cigarette buds and liquor bottles of the travellers lined the perilous alleys that smelt of urine and were musked by desperation. Thick smoke blanketed the rooftops in and an ominous shade hung overhead. Alicia huddled closely with Jaden, as William and Laila went on undeterred. They traveled downhill to the beggars' circle, where many men driven mad by promise writhed in the agony of their avarice. They reached out to grab the children but could not bring it upon themselves, once seeing them travel down the trail to the shanty town.

"What fools are you to descend this trail? Turn back now, this is not the way for mirth and cheer. Murderers line this hall, I being amongst them." A beggar followed after Jaden and Alicia. Wide, round eyes, dinner plates of a serving that they didn't have enough to place. They instantly smelt his malignant odor. Jaden turned in disgust, and Alicia viewed as the man whose bones were visibly imprinting his skin, fell to the ground in shame. Tears falling from his eyes.

"Turn back!" He yelled before dropping to the floor on his knees. The children pressed on through the foul, odious city. A wall collapsed, revealing an empty host of debris and melancholy. There were two bowls sitting upon a dusty table. There was a small, bright-eyed, emaciated boy, shivering over a dish. Alicia slowly got closer and noticed it wasn't a bright-eyed boy but instead a dwarf with cataracts. William and Laila never turned back to look at the collapse and missed Jaden running to defend Alicia as the former pirates-presently beggars, descended upon the pair from every direction.

"You want me to tell you where that guy is?" The burly, hairy-armed pirate examined the image. He squinted at the poster and cleared his throat, looking between William and the paper in disbelief with eyes that recalled an inspiration that had long been dimmed. "That's no man, that's a legend. The father of privateering; the illustrious black hood. The only privateer to ever earn a bounty under contract." The pirate slammed his gun on the table and threw his head back with a laugh. William stared at the man deadpan.

"When they say dead or alive, they don't mean grave robbing!" A slimmer man who wore a dirtied short-sleeved shirt and frayed canvas shorts jested as he pulled a peashooter from his shoe. A few people bumped their mugs on the table, ale swishing around with their uncontrollable laughter. One of the patrons slapped a large, muscular man on the back, but rather than join in the revelry, he gave an acerbic stare and held his drink steady.

"Don't touch me," the muscular man uttered acrimoniously.

"Black Hood, eh? They say that he traveled the world robbing nations of their wealth, overthrew governments- look, this isn't a history lesson. Now get out, and we may just not kill you." All the seated patrons save one all rose at the hairy-armed man's suggestion.

"But first empty those schoolboy pockets." The hairy-armed man announced, rubbing his palms together like a fly on top of filth. Laila looked back at the two men at her rear, blocking the exit. She sighed, turned to the front, popped a comb in her teeth, and began tying back her hair. "You deaf boy?" the man pressed on, tapping William's head. "Hello?" he tapped again.

"Alright." William breathed deeply. The man grabbed him, and William immediately took hold of his hand. There was a coldness to his touch and a glaze over his eyes that suggested he no longer maintained a comfortable facade and exposed the nature that he found himself trying to stray from. The rest of his compatriots were astounded that such a small boy could hold back this goliath force. William grabbed tighter, and unfortunately, the man had already overextended his wrist so that all the boy had to do was force the fingers back with just enough pressure on the back of the palm for the wrist to splinter from the man's skin. CRACK. Laila's head turned slightly toward the sound just as she secured her locks with the comb. Another deafening pop filled the tavern and some men on the level cringed, scrunched their faces, or started checking the flexibility of their own hands. William held the limp, purple hand, feeling the bones snapping underneath as he exerted more force. The other hand came out and struck the man's nose, moving him slightly. Another blow and another step back. Soon the conflict moved them both to the railing, only being directed by a similar series of blows to the man's face. All the patrons downstairs watched attentively as William struck the man's head several times against the railing. Some small piece of brain was left behind as the railing broke, sending the two crashing towards the floor. William got up, leaving the man bloodied on the floor, his face bruised in several areas. Life spilling from the crack in his head. He grabbed hold of the boy's leg with a last reflex reaction, trembling in pain as one palm was purple and disjointed, the other scraped and bloodied. The bloody palm shivered over William's skin. William shook him off and stomped hard on the man's discolored wrist, sending the man into unbearable agony.

"Now, where is he?" William showed the picture at a distance so that everyone could get a good look at his eyes, scanning the room for any trace reactions. Eyes widening, hands fidgeting, maybe even a sip of beer. He adjusted his foot to create a more echoed scream from the man. "Where is he?"

"I don't know," the man admitted, "please, oh god, I don't know," he sobbed. "Please, I don't want to-" He was cut off by the sound of a round drilling deep into his skull.

"Have some dignity." The man who spoke had big hair that was mostly covered by his cotton-laced bicorne cap, and sizable muscles blocked by his jacket, only visible by the veins on his tanned arms. The tanned arm man got out of his seat. Immediately, all the patrons in the bar aimed their weapons at his head. He seemed to be unbothered by the event and continued walking blithely as his footsteps almost moved rhythmically to the sound of various weapons being cocked and readied.

"What is John Coxton doing standing up for some swabby?" The slim man from upstairs kept his weapon drawn. The man walked over to William, who was now crouched in anticipation.

"Relax, kid, I'm not an enemy. I'm your exit ticket." The man leaned over and whispered.

"You're wrong about at least three things!" The man shouted into the tavern.

"He killed our captain. That's wrong, isn't John Coxton supposed to maintain the law of pirates?" The slim man looked to another member of his crew, a more plump member who wore glasses that became mirrored in the light. The glasses man nodded, and had the slim man not been so irate, he would have noticed the man's glasses held a reflection of the entire room. The man next to William noticed.

"That's the one thing you almost got right. John Coxon does maintain the code of buccaneering, unfortunately, this kid isn't a pirate, I sure as hell ain't standing up for him, and my name's Bobby Clarke, not John Coxon."

William stayed alert and took the time to scan the room for Laila, who watched from the broken railing. The man took his pistol and whipped William with it a good time across his forehead. William stumbled and raised his hand to hit the man, but he pointed his gun right towards his chest, once more leaning into his ear. "First lesson, ain't nothing here but a bunch of lying, cheating snakes, don't trust anyone more than you need to, I reckon that lady up there is counting on you making it out of here." William glanced over at Laila, who stood wide-eyed, with a twitch going across the corner of her upper lip. She turned to argue with someone, slowly reaching for the comb in her hair. The man leaned over to William's ear. "Now, lucky you, I hate to upset a beautiful lady, but unluckily, I got a reputation to upkeep." Before William could so much as move a muscle, the gun went off.

CHAPTER 17

"Ah shit," Jaden smacked his palm across the beggar's face. He held onto the head and used it as a pivot to kick another in the ribs. They had all come in droves after him and were almost more than he could handle. He bashed the leg of the one he held onto and threw the beggar to the side.

"Why am I doing this? Why am I wasting time? I need to hurt them badly, and I need to do it quick." He thought to himself, he looked over to his left and to his right, but he couldn't find Alicia. His mind drifted back to the events moments before they separated.

"It's a gaelic, we'll be back on top in no time!" One of the beggars hollered as the host of debris collapsed around the open-air shack. Jaden pushed Alicia just in time, and the hand he covered her arm with now had an icepick sticking from the back of his palm. Alicia shoved the beggar with her shoulder, and he went flying towards the other side. Jaden pulled the pick out and dropped it to the floor with a rattle. He urged them to come near, and they began circling him. Jaden wasn't always prepared to fight, but fortunately, he had long arms. Jaden cocked back his hand, swung his fist and let a beggar have it so bad, there were teeth marks on the back of Jaden's pale hand. This did not deter the group's movement, for instance, as they continued in their delusive discourse.

"All we need is one Gaelic, and we can get a ship off this island."

"One Gaelic is three slaves, or are three slaves one Gaelic?"

"I will help you with the ship, all I want is a hot meal. I've come too far for this treasure." The three men all jumped at Jaden, and they all fell through another wall. Alicia had picked up the ice pick and was nearing the fresh debris when she heard the sound of a gunshot ring out. Still gripping the ice pick tightly, she ran off towards the source of the sound. The dwarf and the other beggars didn't follow her, but they had blocked Jaden's path. Jaden tried not to think of whether any beggars had followed after her, he tried to find a gap where he could slip past, but more and more surrounded any potential of escape. He managed to hold his own for far longer than he thought, but the situation was becoming time-consuming. He whipped out the knife Shiela gave him and screamed like a madman as he plunged it into the ribs of a beggar who lay at his feet. The beggar let out an equally horrified response.

"Wait! Wait! It's pointless to try and kill this boy!" A beggar pushed his way to the front of the crowd.

"Yeah, what that guy said." Jaden tried to pull the knife, but it wouldn't quite come out.

"We don't want him for the hunt, we want him for the coin." One of the original beggars rang out.

"That won't work either," the frontman said.

Jaden put his foot on the man's ribs and pulled, before jiggling the knife a bit, and driving it deeper, almost as if the man's rib cage were a jammed lock.

"I watched the boy die in front of me." The man breathed heavily with the sentiment. The light revealed his face. It was the slender man with the pointed nose, who now had red splotches on his skin, and a face emaciated to where even his jawbone was visible.

"That doesn't sound so bad. I'm sure we can get a good price before-"

"And he took down our first mate along with our captain." The man continued solemnly.

"One of those was not me-ooop- oop." Jaden twisted the knife, tilting his elbow and angling his wrist, but the knife had more or less popped out. The beggars' innards were torn to shreds, but luckily, some form of shock or adrenaline had activated, and he had passed out long before Jaden had carved the knife a path to exit.

"After that, our crew disbanded. Some tried to charter a ship back home, but most of them were consumed by-" The man continued his tale as the beggars all focused their attention towards the story. Jaden had no real desire to hear the entirety of the tale. Now that his knife was secure, he backed his way out the alleyways of the shanty housing. He watched vigilantly for any other signs of detection, but the crowd was truly raptured by the man's storytelling. Backing down the alley, he stumbled on a slope. Jaden turned around and went down the steep incline. He almost slid down when he saw the cloth of Alicia's shirt. He confirmed he was going the right way and proceeded with care down the slope.

"Now, the man you search for, I may be able to find him, but I'll need the help of a native. There's tales that he settled in a remote part of the island, seldom visited by others, renowned for its mystery and dealings with the occult." The man put an air of seriousness about his words.

"What makes you so sure I'm from this island?" William held his shoulder and winced.

"You're wearing a school uniform. Not alotta classrooms round these parts. Listen, it's an old privateers tale that Black Hood buried all his rewards from the government and treasures from nations somewhere on this island."

"I'm only interested in finding Black Hood." William pointed to the paper but quickly jerked back his shoulder and coughed.

"You always pass out like that when you get shot?" The man raised his eyebrow, perking up his head like a dog with a new chew toy, grinning as William stared away from him.

"No kidding. That was your first time?" The man laughed and fell on his back, before bursting into tears. William rose from the dirt patch and walked off.

"If you go after him now, things may just end a bit worse than this time around." The man raised a finger gun, "I'm worth less than he, and I got you clean through, imagine what he'll do. This guy's not around because he doesn't want to be. Big fish like that don't go swimming round less, it's eating all the smaller ones." He lowered his finger gun and picked himself off the ground. William turned around, "Little brown haired girl, have you seen her?" he said, his voice hoarse from holding back a cough.

"Oh yeah, she's safe. I don't miss and I don't have accidents." The man prided himself on the statement.

William twitched with anger and cleared his throat.

"Where is she?"

"Back at the bar waiting with a friend," Bobby put a hand over his mouth and swallowed a laugh.

William surveyed his surroundings. He was near the coast now. The sand wasn't very far off, and the ocean was a much more comfortable view than the tavern they had exited. He couldn't tell how much time had passed since he passed out and awoke to the man splashing seawater over his face.

"I take it you don't take a break at hell often," the man stood up, his pistol gleaming in the faint sunlight. He lifted the top of his hat and began scratching at his head with the barrel.

"Take me back," William twitched once more.

"Not until you do me a little favor, I need you to help me find some guys, less than your big fish, but it'll prove to be some observation of your talent."

"Whatever, just take me back to the bar."

"Whoa! Hold your horses, I left that filly with the most steadfast, capable guys in Monarch Cove." The man holstered his weapon and began walking towards the town.

"Idiocy. No one ever accounts for idiocy." William said, shaking his head and running off in the direction he perceived the man to be headed.

Laila had been slightly worried. She knew from the trajectory of the bullet that William was in no real harm. The knife comb was her best option, but the true apprehension came from knowing William was still with that man. No one but Laila and the two crewmen who were escorting her outside currently saw and lived to tell the story of the man's escape. He had held William after the shooting. This gave him enough of a pause from the shock the crowd experienced. He threw William into a nearby floor patron, and before the patron could so much as react to the incoming unconscious schoolboy, a glass flew, smashing into their face. John- or Bobby- or whoever kicked the leg off the table, and it fell to the side. The men behind him all drew their pistols. John took two more cups and threw them at their faces. Only the cups never reached and exploded in mid-air, pierced by two bullets, launched from Coxon's pistol. At this point, the table was being assailed by bullets, but Bobby, who was exorbitantly resourceful, picked out a compact mirror and began aiming it towards the air. He threw another cup in the air, and before it burst from a bullet, he had managed another look at the only sight that truly mattered. The man with the glasses. There were only three people left on the ground, but they had been incredibly hesitant to draw a weapon if they possessed any. John moved the table a little to the left. He managed to slide it a couple more steps. Eventually, he found it. The reload time. John managed to pluck one from the upper level while blindly giving himself cover fire. He charged towards the bar. Even as he provided cover fire, John's attention remained on the bartender, which proved to be well-earned as a dart came hurtling in his direction, but Bobby's reflexes were much quicker, and with his adrenaline pumping, he caught the dart and hurled it directly into the Bartender's eye socket. The man let out a rageful growl, and his true intention was revealed. The gleam of the metal was all that was seen before Bobby jumped over the countertop and stomped the dart through the back of the man's head. John landed next to the shotgun and blasted a few rounds for more cover fire. The bait worked, and one of the men from downstairs shot at the end of the counter. John crawled to the other end and let out a round into that man's face before ducking. The bullets were flying in every which way, John tried to reflect his mirror off a nearby bottle, but it shattered above his head. He used the mirror to shoot the last guy on the floor and let out a large whistle. In that instant, a man upstairs had his face turned to pulp as the hulking, muscular figure smashed its fist into the side of both his head and cheek. The man would have probably died shortly afterwards, but a bullet through his skull expedited that process. The instant when the men turned to the scene, one of them was plucked by the compact mirror Coxon. The man with the glasses would have pulled the trigger, but suddenly red spurted over the lens, and he dropped the gun, wheezing as he tried to grab at the large scimitar now sticking through his throat.

"We're done here?! " John yelled into the tavern. Only his men answered.

"Aye!" The duo upstairs cheered.

"There's a little girl hiding under the table. You make sure not a drop of harm comes to her. I'll go wake the boy." Those were the last words the man said before he holstered his Lorenzoni repeater pistol with one ball still left in the chamber. He scooped William's unconscious, bleeding body and stepped into parts unknown. Now Laila sat on a barrel outside the tavern, and she could see Jaden approaching as he wildly flailed his arms, in an attempt to look like one of the nearby beggars. Laila released her hair at that moment, she dug the knife comb deep into the barrel and twisted it until a steady flow of ale poured. The man pulled out his gun, and Alicia yelled as she charged with the ice pick. The moment the man aimed the gun towards Alicia, Laila instantly hopped off the barrel. Alicia, still screaming at the top of her lungs, closed her eyes. She tried to arc her hand back as far as possible, imagining her arm was a drawstring, and threw the ice pick with all her might. The pick went straight as an arrow and seemed like it would make it to the tavern, but instead the force of the throw managed to jam the handle in the dirt, a short distance from the entrance. The handle jammed into the dirt. Alicia stopped in place as both her and the man stared at her failed attempt. Scratching his head, unsure whether this was an attack or a package delivery. Laila grabbed the knife from the barrel and slit one of his tendons so quick, the knife almost came out clean. The man grabbed for his leg, still holding tight to his weapon. Jaden had finally come close to the tavern, further than Alicia but not further than the ice pick. The ice pick burrowed into the flesh underneath Jaden's foot, like a pin through gelatin. Jaden hopped and went crashing into the hulking Goliath. Upon landing, the man had proved very little resistance, and Jaden went from holding his foot to holding the gun away as they wrestled and slid across the aisle. They continued to slide through the tavern, the man repeatedly stumbling backwards, and Jaden hopping to defend himself from the weapon. Jaden jumped away just before the goliath tumbled over the broken part of the railing.

"Get that brat!" The goliath hollered out as the rest of his legs crumbled under the impact of the floor. He raised his gun, and at that moment, Jaden ducked and covered his ears. The goliath's gun rang out, and a wiry man who had attempted to cut Jaden's neck looked down at the fresh hole in his chest. The wiry man fell face-first from the balcony, tripping over Jaden and plunging his sword into the mouth of the goliath. Jaden pulled at the pick and twisted it properly before releasing it from his foot.

"Okay, Alicia, you did that on purpose!" Jaden threw in under his breath.

"What are you talking about? I was just trying to help!" Alicia defended.

"Come on, you're like the best one on the archery team, you don't miss," Jaden grumbled.

"I don't have my glasses! I can't aim at all!" Alicia protested.

"Well, you certainly can't aim." Jaden folded his arms, but Alicia failed to catch the sentiment as she gazed into the bar. There were blurs of red, black, and brown. She moved in closer, crunching glass shards underneath her shoes and saw the proliferated tables knocked over. She walked over to the broken bannister and focused intently on a pinkish, green, and black blur, only to see the owner with a dart pin through his eye. Pinned to the board. The unsightly scene welled her eyes with tears. More of the red and brown blurs came into focus, and she realized one was a dead body. A man with his eyes shut and proliferated a little less than the table. Once she realized the first blur was a corpse, the room began to come more into focus, and she could see the corpses surrounding her, as a shiver built and her breathing ceased. Jaden peered over at this, quickly grabbed her and slowly walked her out of the bar. Her sobbing had grown to an uncontrollable rage, and she beat Jaden at the floor of the entrance. She whacked him once to the ground, and he looked sideways in shame. Her eyes immediately welled up once more, and she dove to the floor to hold him. He laughed it off and helped her back to her feet. Laila sat pouting. Droplets of ale falling from her shoe as she waited atop the barrel, watching Jaden and Alicia come towards her, but she had no interest at all in anything they could have to say. They truly couldn't provide her any relief and would only serve as more white noise. The smiles on their faces are what made it truly difficult to deny them the reaction they so clearly desired. She attempted to hide her expression, looking in another direction.

"Laila!" Alicia shouted, latching onto the girl.

"Laila!" Jaden shouted, bringing his face a little too close for Laila's comfort. She put her hand over his face, halting their proximity.

"God, the pirates have more decency, you hear me? Pirates.." Her frustration grew in that moment. Jaden released the girl from his grasp immediately, "I have decency."

"Not much," Laila added.

"You know I'm not sure I like-"

"Hey, leave those girls alone!" A man shouted from a distance.

"Have to at least question some of what you're doing if the pirate man's telling you that," Alicia chided. She nearly fixed her glasses, but then put her two fingers down and sighed.

"No way.." The man's gruff voice got closer.

"It's okay, he's with-" William tried to relay before the sound of a gunshot rang off, and Jaden stopped in his tracks. Jaden reached for his head, but barely made it to his shoulder, before the hand collapsed along with his body. Alicia slapped her hand over her eyes with a blood-curdling, horrified scream. She fell to the floor sobbing. Laila was ecstatic. His bloody bits of brain showered the floor, and his vibrant eyes now lay devoid of any life.

"How can you people just do things like that?" She abandoned Jaden's body and ran at the man who stood steps away from the entrance. She looked back at Laila, who clapped excitedly and laughed with her fists pumping the air, almost cheering the massacre. This offset Alicia, who shuddered in fear as Jaden's corpse dissolved into the dark opening that seemed to spread over his body parts. His clothes remained, but the sight of the boy had been completely lost. It was at that moment, William came unfazed up the footing of the level, Laila rejoicing.

"William!" Laila cried out half in disbelief. There was some relief to her expression, but that slowly washed away as she caught the blood wet enough to make his shirt cling to his skin. Alicia fell to the floor, "Why?" was all she could manage and then she saw it from the corner of her tear-filled eye. Fiery red hair appeared from a little below the hill. He motioned over to Alicia and tapped her head.

"Shadows don't die dumb dumb." He then cooled down to where his clothes lay and put a shirt over his tall, lean figure.

"You children are maddening," the man took the words straight from Alicia's mouth and brought with it a new bliss. Her over-contemplative nature had led her to thoroughly analyze her friends' mentality. They weren't scared of death, but not out of sheer madness. They had accepted it, grown accustomed to the casual coming and goings of family members and friends. A great tragedy had washed their minds black and made their conscience full. Death was no more of an acquaintance than she was. He walked with these children. The scythe held to their neck that could rip them from this mortal coil at any moment had become their skin. Death amounted to another predetermined script that they could find their own way to interpret. She saw Laila's jeers at Jaden, William's solemn grumbling, and Jaden's own hapless musings and stood next to the dark harbinger, grabbing them all tighter and closer than she had done anything in her entire life.

"Neat little bunch you kids have here, maybe this task won't be as difficult as I made it to be." The man interjected, dulling their youthful expressions.

"I made a deal to help this guy kill some people," William stated plainly.

"Wow, just shouting it out there, ay boyo." The man laughed a hearty laugh.

"Why?" Alicia asked plainly.

"He saved my life and whatever." William shrugged.

"One bullet to the shoulder knocked him out, but you should see what I did to the rest of the room, did ya?" The man let out a robust laugh, his eyes streamed with tears, and he took in all the dark that surrounded him.

"So now I gotta go help him kill more people," William said blankly. He sighed deeply, glanced over at Laila and looked at the man. The man met William's gaze and began.

"There's a ridge not far from here. I can lead you up to it, just those who are coming, keep up, and those who aren't, keep away from peddlers." The dismal breeze sent chills down their spines; they had grown accustomed to the hellish debauchery that was this cove, but by no means had they become comforted. William bounded off after the man. Jaden threw on some pants and followed next. Laila and Alicia looked at each other worriedly and continued after the group. They continued walking down the shanty town roads until William let out a large groan.

"What's wrong?" Alicia asked immediately and, upon seeing William grab at his shoulder, uttered a soft "Oh yeah."

"Hey, I think we should stop and find a doctor," Laila announced.

"No, I'm alright." William coughed and squeezed his injury tighter.

"He says he's alright, I say we push on, leads tend to grow cold if you don't keep up the heat." The man gruffed and kept pace.

"Nonsense!" Jaden slapped William's back, and he coughed some blood onto the floor.

"You've been through way worse; this is nothing." Jaden held on to William, and when he let go, William nearly toppled over before Jaden put his hand back and stood the boy upright.

"I missed all the vitals; it went clean through. He'll walk it off." John protested. Laila and Alicia ran over to help Jaden support William. Laila took hold of his shoulder and inspected it, while Alicia and Jaden hovered over the boy. John tried to keep himself away from the scene, but his natural curiosity got the best of him, and he ended up hovering over the children.

"What, what's going on?" John inquired.

Jaden held a semi-conscious William in his arms, crouching down so the boy's weight wouldn't tip him. Alicia covered her mouth in terror, and Laila looked up with bloodstained hands.

"He isn't doing well, he's bleeding really badly. I can patch him up, but he'll need some water. Drinkable water." Laila rested her palms flat on William's body.

"Water, I can do. Shit should have thought of that one. You all hang tight here, patch the boy up, I'll run and grab some fluid." John said. He ran a short distance to some nearby trees and wrapped his jacket around the trunk. Stepping on a ridge, he shimmied himself up towards the top.

"Take off the shirt. We don't have much time." Laila folded her arms and tapped her foot impatiently.

"You know when people say like get a room. This is what they mean." Jaden's face scrunched in disgust as he covered his eyes and spaced the gaps so that he could catch a glimpse of William removing his shirt without protest.

"Should I um turn around?" Alicia asked, averting her eyes.

"You're still looking?" Jaden voiced his disbelief, shading his eyes, before taking another peak. Laila grabbed both ends of the wound and examined the hole left behind.

"I don't trust this guy at all, but he wasn't lying about the shot, it's clean through. Okay, what's the game plan?" Laila's hyper-focused expression immediately dissolved.

"We have to get rid of him, he knows about the village. We'll stick with him until we find an opening. You two should head back." William's eyes instantly opened, and all strain from his voice disappeared.

"Why don't we just all head back? We're all tired. William got shot, and the bounty isn't even here, so maybe we just cut our losses." Alicia offered innocently.

"That's a big no can do with a side of been there done that," Jaden crossed his arms and nodded.

"Jaden's right. We can't risk any pirates knowing about the village. This isn't a game." William coughed.

"At least let me patch you up. He really didn't hit any vitals, but still, it's gotta hurt." Laila held William's arm up.

"Hey, he's coming back down the tree. If anyone's getting out of here now would be the time." Jaden crouched to the group's level to hide his words.

"Go, we'll say you went to find medical supplies, you remember the way back, right?" William drew his arm back.

"William, this isn't your average pirate. Be careful." Laila wiped the blood on the dirt and dusted the clods onto the ground.

"What? Don't think I can take him?" William raised his eyebrows.

"Maybe if both his hands were busy… and you caught him by surprise." Laila deadpanned, entirely serious.

"I'll keep that in mind."

— CHAPTER 18 —

The swampy marshlands were by no means better than the rustic shanty town, and the air now stank of something much more foul than common malice.

"You know, for the supposed hellish reputation that place holds, I'd say it's not that bad over there. I think I could be a pirate." Jaden moved the vine from his face, "in and out of hell and only died once." He slowly let in his sense of self-satisfaction. "Yes!" Jaden wrestled himself free from the vine, and the man moved to the side, while William jumped away from the snap that echoed across the murky stillness. William grimaced at him as he gently hopped over the branch and into the muck. It splashed about as much as if a raindrop had hit the area, but that had no effect on the mud and rot that had already been creeping into his footwear.

"What's on you?" Jaden rehashed, reaching up to pull at a tree branch.

"Nothing, just keep it moving. God, this place is truly god-awful, isn't it? Why, I swear this swamp was not visible from the bay." The man walked through, feet sinking each time into the muck, cuffs covered in the grime of the marsh. "Where is this damn ridge?" He groaned.

"Wait, is that an actual question, or are you just saying question words in sentences again?" Jaden let the branch go, letting it snap the man on the back of his head, slightly raising his hat.

"It's just up this way," William reassured.

They passed the final swamp-covered trees. Thick veins filled with harmful sludge spun around the trunk like streamers on a column. Even the roots looked alive, their green arteries pulsating through the earth.

"We can't just go home, it was hard enough finding this place, and we're this close to the captain's stash," they heard from underneath the ridge. They quickly hurried to the edge of the marsh where the vines had been slashed.

"Listen, I'm sure we can find another way. We couldn't go home before, but now we can charter a ship. Let's bring home some other fortune. "

"No… I can't just abandon this, it's been years since I've seen my wife or son. We take the captain's stash or his head. That's the only fortune we're taking home."

The two voices went back and forth for a while.

"Probably old bounty hunters looking to make a quick buck just like you, kid." The man patted William on his back. "Seems they've realized they're outclassed, but they know a little something about your friend, might be worth giving a look into. Unless, of course, there's some other island fortune?" The man gave William a little push, then adjusted his own trousers. William drudged forward, up the clearing, and Jaden stood doe-eyed in bewilderment at his best friend's sudden compliance. William waved his hand and Jaden fell back to watch the boy in his nature.

"You went where?!" Ephriam bellowed into the hills, "I can't believe you two! That snake pit is quite literally the most dangerous place in the world."

"We know," the two girls said in annoyed unison.

"The worst of the worst can only be found there; no good can come from going there."

"We made it back," Alicia stated plainly before nonchalantly turning to High-five Laila.

"Hey Ephriam, have you ever been over there?" Laila asked.

"One time, it was back when this town first started developing. I had gone to the circles of thieves-" Laila and Alicia snuck off in the middle of his speech. They snuck into the back of Odette's sweetshop and gorged themselves on sugary treats, courtesy of the owner and the obvious appeal of youth.

"Do you think they're okay?" Alicia asked, a spoonful of sugared toffee, hovering above her plate.

"If they weren't, we couldn't do anything about it," Laila said, sipping her hot chocolate. Her brow slightly frowning. Laila looked down at her skirt and glared at it for a second. Just as she raised her head, Alicia turned to the window.

"Hey, look! It's Saphron!" she pointed.

"So," Laila shrugged, letting go of her skirt.

"She's in our class, we could at least acknowledge that," Alicia let the spoon clink across the plate, the toffee now residue on the utensil.

"C'mon," Alicia grabbed Laila's arms, and much to Laila's surprise, she managed to stand up from

her seat gracefully. Movements jerking as they got closer to the door, and the unfamiliar social dominion. Before she knew it, they had completely halted.

"Hey, Saphron!" Alicia screamed out the door of the shop. The girl pretended not to hear and kept walking. "Saphron!" She called out again, her enthusiasm either matching or increasing slightly.

"Saphron!" she bellowed into the crowd.

"What is it!" Saphron stopped mid-drudge to respond, her tone filled with an acerbic bitterness, keeping hints of discontent.

"Come eat with us," Alicia motioned to the door. Laila stood frozen, she swallowed her confidence, took a deep breath and sat down in her seat. Alicia returned, leading the girl into the sweet shop and sitting her down beside the table. Laila composed herself and looked at Saphron, her low-cut hair that curled around her neck, her smooth chin, thin, straight lips that never rounded out, but nonetheless brought out the fullness of her cheeks and sharp, pointed nose.

"Might as well sit with people who aren't Guilliam or Cadence." Alicia searched for a connection. Saphron sighed deeply and stood up from the chair. Laila watched wide-eyed at the girl as she slammed the table and chewed Alicia out for five continuous minutes. The unbridled scorn of a passion tainted by spoiled promise. Expectations of womanhood, as well as the solidarity within those expectations. Performances of identities long ago resolved for the purposes of maintaining any semblance of normalcy outside of inner turmoil. The scorn, shame, and ridicule that were birthed from her own narrative being ripped from her control. These incendiary offenses, both internal and external, had been habitually extinguished by Saphron until Alicia chose to make her remark. Now all these dimmed feelings lit up a resentment which burned away at her restraint and by proxy her own perceived self-image. She watched Alicia sit astonished, listening to every platitude and veiled insult that could express her emotions without revealing intention. It was truly the first time since feeling for someone else that Saphron was able to feel something for herself.

"And I think that's just about it, I'm not hurt or upset. There's nothing for us to talk about, there's nothing else that we really have in common. We don't need to be friends or even bond, and especially not over this, try to have some self-respect." Saphron turned around, before Alicia could react, let alone respond. Saphron continued her prideful solitary exit, holding her head high, back straight, using only small, brisk, necessary movements. Alicia slunk back into her chair and put her head down, before her eyes popped right back up with a dazed look.

"Well, that was interesting," Alicia let out, watching through the window as Saphron fumed away.

" I still don't really understand it," Laila admitted whilst nibbling on her Honey milk bar.

"I don't really know if I should be talking about it… She lost. It feels more awkward to express how she feels than to just play along with everything."

"Oh, is that what it feels like to lose?"

They sat quietly, munching on their treats, watching the doorway and all the passersby with vacuous glances.

THWACK! The slender, mustached man's nose shifted out of position with the last punch. Blood spurted into his facial hair and smeared on his palm when he grabbed at the area.

"All we know is what you know." The tan-armed man who had been accompanying William answered calmly.

"Okay, okay," the raggedy, slender mustached man replied.

"We don't know much… Honest!" Answered a short, stocky malcontent. Jaden pressed the blade to his throat so that a rivulet formed as he spoke, "Cabin boys, that's all we were, swabbed the deck, supplied the liquor and the occasional extortion."

"See, this is more than you were telling me before; now we're getting somewhere. Maybe you can tell me without us having to hurt your friend." The tan-armed man smiled genially.

"When the crew disbanded, we were already holding influence in several nations and were well off-"

"Unchallenged as members of the most fearsome gang to rule the seas, our rank went without question." The short, stocky man continued. "Well, it was a bit questioned when-"

"We've sent several envoys to this location, not one has returned. We're here to manage this source of rebellion and put an end to it." The man spoke quickly, glancing over to the compatriot he interrupted. William dismounted, and the slender man thrust the knife towards the boy's chest.

"Fucking kid really messed up my nose." Despite the evasion, the man kept the knife pointed at William, rubbing at what used to be his nose. It took a short roundhouse, but the man was disarmed. From then on, a snap kick hit his head, and his skull dropped to the ground.

"My god," he blustered. "I'm gonna fucking kill this brat." The slender man seized his head in agony, his hair becoming dyed with the small effusion from his skull. William planted his foot firmly on the slender man's cheek. He watched him with ferocious intent, and the man was momentarily paralyzed.

"Jericho, tell them," the short, stocky man fell to his knees in weariness.

"This is so nerve-wracking, sorry man just can't keep my hands still," Jaden had poked the short man's neck several times with the blade so that now the top of his blouse remained bloodied and sticky.

"Don't hurt Burt! We saw our captain," Jericho responded hurriedly, "he's on this island." William brought the picture from his pocket and unrolled the image.

"This man?" William questioned. The hooded cloak-like material was enough, even if there was no clear image of his face, both men's eyes widened.

"Yes! He's the one who stole treasure from the world's wealthiest nations! At the end of this village, there's a-" the slender man gulped. BOOM! William jumped back as the shot rang out. He heard the choking of blood and tears coming from the other man, the body jolting with the bullet's collision. "That's all I needed to hear," the man let out, "come, boys."

"Wait! They know where the treasure is!" William tried to appeal, but it was too late. The man spun the repeater off his finger, and Jaden let go of Burt's body before a hole went through the stocky man's head and his body slammed in the field, sailing dandelion blowballs into the breeze.

"What the hell, man? They knew the person who hid the treasure! They've actually met Black Hood!" William protested, looking back and forth between the men with almost identically placed holes on their foreheads.

"Weren't you listening, kid? It's at the end of a village. Eesh, if you're slowing down this much, maybe we should get some shuteye, let's-"

"No! They know Black Hood, they'll be able to tell us who it was that buried the treasure!" William expressed as he racked his brain for the man's thought process.

"Kid, that's Jericho Burgess and Burt Stay. I've been tracking Black Hood's band so long I'm basically part of the crew. There's only one village I haven't checked.

Alicia wouldn't have caught it if the mirth of her laughter hadn't overtaken her. When she opened her eyes, a small glimpse caused her to dramatically swing her head around. She pulled Laila to the floor. "Look." She pointed. Guilliam and Cadence sat hand in hand on the branch, waiting for the sunset. They needed no words; the moment was made entirely their own. Cadence looked up at Guilliam briefly, but it was enough; he caught her chin and pulled her close. Their lips met with the orange-tinted sky, and with its parting, the sun shone with such fulgence that one glare was enough for Alicia to bury her eyes in one of her arms. Laila squinted, and it must've been out of the corner of her eye, but she watched Cadence's hand crawl across the branch before being snatched up by Guilliam as they waited for the sun to disappear over the bounds of their over-arching branch.

Laila got off the floor and dusted herself off. She had intruded on their moment long enough. "What are you doing?" Alicia urged.

"Trust me, they won't notice us," Laila pressed on.

"Oh," Alicia bumbled, rising casually to her feet.

"Jaden and William have been gone a while; it's almost sundown." Alicia let out her concern.

"They disappear for days all the time, sometimes it's weeks," Laila grumbled.

"Wow."

"I know," she responded.

"That's annoying."

"That's William," she said reflexively.

The swamp had proven to be a bit much for William and his company. The muck they were leaving behind seemed more conspicuous than exploratory, and where the grime hardened, uncomfortable itching began to spread. These were the reasons the trio had decided it would be best to call it a night, and without a beach or river to wash themselves off at, they all headed to an inn nearby Monarch Cove to prepare themselves for the morning's journey. They had checked into the inn, and before they were even shown to the room, the innkeeper showed them to the bath. He collected all of their things and closed the door. About a minute or two later, he heard a knock before the door opened.

"There are other guys in here." William peeked his head out.

"Such a charming young man, look at you, so precious and naive." The innkeeper put his hand over a blush, and William slunk back into the room, disgruntled. After they had collected their things, the innkeeper showed them all to one room. The old man instinctively grabbed a chair and put himself in it. He kept fully dressed and slung his bag over the side, his pistol in full view.

"If there's anything, I mean anything I can do for you boys, don't be afraid to holler."

"Can we get another bed?" Jaden requested.

"Only if you're paying for another room." The innkeeper flipped his feather scarf. It seemed to be made of an assortment of the island's birds rather than dyed materials. After a moment of silence, he quietly revoked his offer by closing the door.

"I can take the floor," William positioned his back towards the front of the door. This gave him a good view of the surroundings. From his vantage point, he could see the entirety of the room. The little window that hung over the bed. The painting on the wall of a variety of fruits and, most importantly, the chair where the man sat, and left the engraved steel pistol hanging over the side. Giving his aim a similar vantage point to the one William took.

"Alright, guess I'm taking the bed." Jaden slumped off to bed. He opened his eyes, the blazing heat forcing them into an unforgiving light. He rolled on his side and jolted the two awake. "Well, now, we can get going?" the man yawned, scratching his chest, sluggishly gathering his belongings.

"So we shall," William rose slowly from the ground. He stayed up all night waiting for an opening. Morning came before an opportunity. Well, there was one moment in the dead of the night when William saw the man's eyes close while he held tight to his bag and the arm of the chair. William crept over to Jaden and pulled the knife from the boy's pocket. He drew the knife sharply and nicked Jaden's finger with the blade. Before the wound could create even one drop of blood, darkness filled the cut, and the flesh mended itself without so much as a mark. William slunk over to where the man was sleeping, blissfully relaxed on the chair. William held the knife over the man's chest. He would plunge it into the man's heart, end the whole affair and return home. The man would never make it back to the village, and there'd be one less person in this world who could help him understand his tragedy. He knew it was selfish, immature, reckless, and irresponsible, but William also knew helping this man find this treasure would lead to the culprit behind the village's destruction and ultimately his parents' murder. Regretfully, he stowed the knife back into Jaden's pocket and laid on the floor attempting to justify his own rationale to himself until the light of day spilled into his eyes. William twisted the air above the doorknob before reaching down to open the door. There in his face stood a small girl, who must've been half his age, holding a silverware tea set. She froze up long enough for William to walk past her. His clothes smelt of dirt and perspiration. That's what it always came to anyway. Laila would help him with the laundry like she always did. It would be nice; he felt more of an urge to go home. His walk became brisk, and as he reached the foothold of the stairs, a dusty little servant girl appeared in front of him.

"Um, would you like tea?" The girl asked demurely.

"Wait up!" Jaden called from the end of the hall, the little girl turned around to the long, lanky limbs that resembled a scarecrow being stretched until it thinned. The figure gave her such a start, one of the porcelain cups fell off the tray, but instantaneously was caught by the man with the jacket and revolver. He placed it back in its original position.

"Excuse me, little miss," John patted her head. "We won't be having time for any tea." The man mussed her hair and proceeded down the stairs, his holster and assortments jangling down the descent. William shrugged and followed suit. The fiery-haired boy appeared from a distance, snatched a scone, and dashed to join with his cohorts. The girl held the tray, still watching the now-empty space at the end of the stairs. William rushed back in an instant, and the little tea kettle and cups jumped off the plate. Jaden came shortly afterwards, but the startle had settled.

"I feel like if you actually tried to get some sleep, you wouldn't be so forgetful."

"Shut the hell up. Little girl, where are you from? Have you seen other kids anywhere?" William bent his knees to speak to the servant girl, but she backed away, without speaking, holding out her tray.

"You're scaring her, William!" Jaden yelped, matching the girl's nervousness. "See, I told you," Jaden grabbed William's arm and pulled him to the side.

"What are you doing?" William questioned.

"We're not kids anymore, you're basically a random grown-up yelling at her, let me try." Jaden turned around, and William begrudgingly followed. "Little girl," Jaden coughed.

"Where are your momma and papa right now?" Jaden widened his eyes, raised his nose, and hung his mouth open just enough for his razor-sharp teeth to be visible. The girl immediately started crying and dropped her arms to the side so quickly, the plate hovered for a while before William snatched it out of the air, still balancing the rattling dishes.

"Jaden, what the absolute hell? Sorry about that, my name's William." William balanced the platter until the cups steadied.

"We just want to know if you were born here, what's your name?" William crouched with the dish.

"Cindy." The girl said through slow sobs while she rubbed her eyes.

"Hi Cindy, where are your parents from?" William tried to speak softly.

"I don't know! I wasn't born here!" The girl bawled louder.

"That's okay, that's okay, Cindy. How'd you get to the island?"

"I don't remember! My parents said I was a baby when I was on the ship." Cindy whined.

"William, come on, let's go, nobody's being kidnapped." Jaden grabbed William's shoulder.

"I'm sorry. I'm sorry." William rushed out several times in softer tones until the girl began to calm down. "Here's your tea. You can serve your tea." William passed the tray back to Cindy, and she gripped it, despite the dishes rattling to a cacophony more unbearable than her wailing. William put a hand on her shoulder and leaned in with the same soft tone. "We just wanted to make sure that there weren't bad guys, um, keeping kids in cages." At the end of William's statement, the girl entirely dropped the tea set to the ground with a crash, and ran past the two bawling louder than she ever had prior.

"Oh god, I feel dumb." William slapped his face.

"Isn't it nice?" Jaden put a consoling hand on William's back.

"What are you talking about?"

"Welcome to my world. I mess up all the time, even when I'm trying. It's nice to just be wrong sometimes. Making mistakes is one of the most human things you can do. That's something you and Laila don't really get to do, just mess up and be wrong. Being smart sounds nice, but I can't imagine that pressure, or I could, but I'd probably be wrong."

Alicia stared out the window. The absence of her friends had drifted her thoughts further and further away from the lesson. Laila had not come to school, but that was no surprise considering the frustrations she had vented the prior night. This left Alicia to explore the classroom, almost as if she had started an entirely new school. Bryce had been there before both Alicia and the teacher. He bit into an early morning apple that shone like the anally retentive boy had wiped it clean. The next person came, Venna, she dragged her feet and an air of misery into the classroom. Sieya, Dayvonna, and Francine all came together, speaking almost to a shouting level about their weekend's events. Not long afterwards came Chesney Adams and his cousin Kerrigan, who furtively searched for the teacher as they relayed their paranoia to one another. Kerwin and Anthony walked proudly and greeted the class as they took their seats and immediately fell into discourse. Susanna arrived shortly after, greeted the entire class with a general salutation and fell in with the other natives. Otto, Tran, and Lofly looked overly haggard for having spent a weekend away from classes, but that could have been due to the independent practice they had been obsessively engaging in that had driven Alicia to more solitary pursuits such as archery. Alicia turned her head away from them before she caught their attention. She let her mind wander into possibilities of reconciliation, but each plan felt more flawed than the last.

"Alicia, can you keep your eyes to yourself? You're making me uncomfortable." Bryce moved the cloth from his apple and tried to duck away from Alicia's view.

"Oh, I'm sorry. " Alicia turned away and created a visor over her eyes.

"I thought you were about to pounce at me, I can't tussle too well with the surgery." Bryce chuckled to himself.

"Bryce, why would I want to hurt you?" Alicia questioned, now looking at Bryce with a frustrated incredulity,

"You don't remember? That thing that happened with my first lo- I mean, your ex?" Bryce nearly popped out of his seat, turning to question.

"Bryce, I was like eleven, I barely remember my ex." Alicia laughed off the memory.

"That's not a luxury I can afford. What happened with him, just all of it, changed everything for me forever. Now I'm just supposed to forget it all. I was positive he would never do something like this, but I could never get a read on that boy." Bryce's lip quivered as he inhaled a soft despair.

"Honest to God Bryce, we're not together. We broke up and haven't been seeing each other since." Alicia put a hand on her desk and looked earnestly into the boy's eyes.

"Bullshit Silverstone, you were just with him the other day. I saw you two after school!" Bryce raised in a harsh whisper not breaking eye contact.

"Bryce, I only hung out with him because of Laila. Jaden and I are over. He is still my ex. I've moved on genuinely, and it feels great. We were all only kids, maybe you should try the same."

Alicia turned her head and stared longingly at the door when her eyes met with another's narrow and green. She immediately turned to her desk.

"Excuse me," Ephriam put one leg up and hopped over Saphron.

"Now, class, turn your page to-"

"I think we got off on the wrong foot," Alicia leaned over to Saphron's seat and by default, the front of the room.

"Well, yea cause you're always speaking from your privilege," Bryce responded.

"I'm sorry if I assumed things. Thank you for expressing that to me. I appreciate you giving me an idea of what's going on. I know that wasn't easy. I want you to know it's okay to feel your feelings. They're your feelings, and nobody should be judging you for having them," she let out softly, turned towards Saphron speaking in her general direction, while neglecting to make eye contact.

Bryce saw the sincerity in Alicia's eyes, and it moved him in ways he didn't yet understand.

"I can't do this right now," he got up and stormed out of the classroom.

"Oh no, we're not doing this again!" Ephriam leapt up, chasing after him.

Alicia turned her head, confused, staring at the empty desk. She looked a little aside from Bryce's vacancy when she caught Saphron staring, who ducked her head almost immediately.

"And I want you to know that love wasn't wasted, it will find its way back to you. Even if it isn't with that person. I'm sorry." Alicia let out once more, now giving her attention wholly to the girl. Saphron kept her head hanging and dropped her things on her desk.

"I'm sorry I unloaded so much on you. You just can't let anything bother you on this island, they're all looking for an excuse to see you how they've always seen you and especially after that. Well, thanks for letting me get that out." Saphron mumbled everything but the last part under her breath. "You're not half-bad," she rolled her eyes with a grumble, not loud enough for anyone to hear except Alicia, who focused intently on the girl the entire time.

"What's that about? How great I am? Didn't catch it?" she smiled, funneling a hand over her ear.

"Don't push it, Silverstone." Saphron accidentally let out a small chuckle, before her face straightened to her usual calloused, unreachable look. Guilliam and Cadence walked in next. Alicia looked over at Saphron with worry.

"Hey, so it seems like Ephriam was on his way out. Does anyone know what's going on?" Guilliam held Cadence's hand as they stood near the doorway.

"He went after Bryce," Kerrigan answered plainly.

"Yeah, he'll probably catch up soon. Bryce hasn't moved the same after his injury." Venna answered matter-of-factly.

"Yeah, but he's definitely going to get distracted by William or some shit. I heard they dropped him in a cave last time." Cadence announced to the class. There was a moment of silence as they all took in the new information. After a while, the rustling of books and chairs could be heard as the students prepared themselves for their departure.

"You know, Laila and I were friends way back- at least I thought we were, before we ever got moved up to this class." Saphron stayed in her seat, looking up at the board.

"You should come hang out with us sometime!" Alicia gathered her things and placed them in her bag.

"Yeah, maybe, it was a while ago. I don't even think she remembers. Watch yourself, Silverstone. That girl moves fast, and she'll outpace you before you realize you fell behind." Saphron sighed.

"Thanks, Saphron. I still think you should come hang with us sometime."

"I'll take you up on that, you know Ephriam would have been back by now if he found Bryce..."

"You're right! I'll go let them know we're hanging today!" Alicia hopped up from her seat.

"Wait, Silverstone- '' Saphron directed her gaze towards Cadence, and the girl's eyes darted askance, the instant she met Saphron's eyes. "Never mind, I'll catch up with you."

"Okay, we're here," the man stood tall. "Okay, boys, here's what's going to happen: you're gonna go up to that door, give it a heavy-handed knock, and when he comes out, I'll unload Mr. Flint."

"Wait, just a minute!" Jaden stared with disbelief at the old moss-covered wall. "This renegade captain, the one who's been charged with murder, smuggling, and overthrowing established governments, lives in this specific rinky-dink tavern?"

"Oh, so it is a tavern?" The man twirled his revolver. "Good eye kid." He holstered the weapon. "Now get knocking."

William walked grudgingly up the steps of the old bar house. He breathed in deeply, and before he could knock, he immediately jumped back. The door flung open, having been blasted by the old, rusted shotgun. The sound echoed over the area and the beach. It was early enough in the day that there weren't too many sounds, and the echo of a gunshot was a familiar sound on the island. "What do the words' banned for life 'mean to you?" Walter aimed his shotgun at William's body.

"Drop the gun." The man now held William with his pistol to the boy's temple.

"I know you." Walter peered into his eyes. "Boys, you've managed to get yourselves mixed up in the worst thing you could be involved with. The gov-."

"Can it be Black Hood you'd never miss. Where's the treasure?" He tugged on William, who looked unamused by this all.

"Man fuck you," William stated, but the man kept his cool.

"I don't wanna kill this kid, but I will." The man pressed the steel to William's head.

"Okay, just calm down." Walter negotiated, lowering the shotgun to the ground.

"No, fuck you, Walter man. All these years, all this time? Just how many died in the Coco bay killings? Or the massacre of Knoll Hill? That fire in Pimento valley..." His words seemed to trail off. The man hit William at the top of his head with the brunt of his pistol, sending a pain quivering down his spine and leaving his body numb.

"Dude, what the hell, that's no way to treat your partners," Jaden remarked

The man scoffed, and William glared at Jadens' idiocy.

"We were never partners, there was never any choice in this for any of you. The treasure is mine and mine alone."

"From the minute he *rescued* me, I assumed as much." William relayed dizzily.

The man grunted heartily. "Fuck you," William said, less dazed.

"Where the fuck is the treasure captain?"

The man kept hold of William, and William kept his arms up in submission. That didn't stop him from raising his pistol to bludgeon the boy once more. Thwack. Laila had gotten there a little bit after the group. She had kept herself close to the familiar spots they all hung around. Neglecting to even go to school in hopes of noticing some semblance that they had made it back to the town. She had heard the shotgun blast and immediately went to investigate. She saw the man hold the gun to William's head and maneuvered around the bushes, waiting for her opportunity. Once his gun was raised for another pistol whip, she saw an opportunity.

"John Coxon. Privateer. What's a pirate go for nowadays? Handful of emeralds, a tiger's eye seems-" Walter was cut off as the awe of the moment entirely stunned his speech.

Laila rushed out of the bushes holding her textbook like a spear. Laila was much shorter than the man, but the textbook was long, and once she held her arms over the top of her head, she was able to almost make the difference. It was truly William's stature that created a convenient vantage for Laila that forced Coxon to crouch lower, and before the man's hand had been brought down, Laila struck at the back of his neck with the corner of her book. The pistol bounced off William's head, and the man fell to the floor with the impact of the large manuscript. He had managed to open an eye when the next hit came to the back of his head, and after a quick flutter, that eye was also shut. Laila raised the book as high as her reach would extend and brought the corner down on the man's skull, crushing it more and more with each blow. Holding the bloodied manuscript with one hand, she dropped it and let it fall onto the man's corpse.

"Give us the treasure." William now held the pistol at Walter, who stood a couple of feet apart from him.

Walter laughed. "Now Ephriam done taught you a lotta things,"

William fired a round as Walter took a step, not even a moment did he falter, slowly approaching while William fired several more.

"But I'm positive firearms ain't one of em." Walter reached for the gun, and William forced it under the man's chin, tip-toeing to track his aim.

"True, but I don't think I'll miss from this range." William twisted the barrel against Walter's skin, prompting him to laugh once more.

"Give us the treasure, Walter," William said. Walter took hold of William's arm, lowering himself onto the barrel. William closed his eyes and took a deep breath.

"Oh, we're definitely sending you kids to jail." Ephriam came from behind the bushes. It took him a little bit longer than Laila to reach the source of the gunshot. He had just caught up with Bryce and almost had his hands on the boy when he heard the familiar voice of one of his students and mechanically wandered towards the sound. He saw the dangerous company surrounding the boys and tried to judge their direction, rather unsuccessfully, as he scoped out the area they were moving towards. Therefore, he missed the preceding hostage situation and only had awareness of the grisly murder at his feet. "What are you doing? Why do you have a gun pointed at Walter William?" It was all he could manage to keep the gun pointed and his attention focused.

"He started all of this. I'm just going to end it. This horrible island, every single misdeed brought upon us, it's all him and his riches." William lamented acrimoniously.

"Oh, you terrible, terrible children. Maybe if you'd open that trace evidence you call a textbook once in a while, we could have skipped this predicament."

"No witnesses!" Jaden screamed as he pulled a blade on Ephriam, only to trip over his own foot. Plunging the blade securely in the ground. "No-" he attempted to say while tugging the blade from the dirt. "No wit-" He grunted while pulling at the handle. "Okay, fine, one witness."

"For the love of god, open the fucking textbook," Ephriam yelled.

— CHAPTER 19 —

THE EPIC OF EPHRIAM
PREFACE

History is written by the victors. That is a story that has been told time and time again. But I never lose! History should be written by me! Take my account of history and learn the truth of this world. Experience for yourself how champions view the passage of time. There are two sides to every story, but only mine matters and actually makes any difference. Through my tale, you will come to understand everything you should hold significant, and everything that is imperative to your survival on this island and the larger world outside of its borders. To learn the past is to learn one's place in the world. We are grateful that we have a chronicle of our times to guide future generations and beyond. The scribes throughout the ages did their best to recreate the events leading up to our times, but they're wrong. This is the truest account of history. A firsthand account of the epochs and periods that have birthed many of our ideas and practices. It has been recorded in time as such an essential document that it is even being taught in the curriculum of the island as essential material. Most people die if they step on this island and don't read this book. The information in it has been deemed vital for survival. They're teaching it in schools! The text is leading future generations! That's history! I win! Again! This is a story of love, it is a story of sickness, friendship, crowns and coups. This is history as it happened. No edits or addenda.

To be continued in… Episode of Ephriam

CHAPTER 20

Ephriam's prolix might've taken a number of characters longer to read than Laila, who herself decoded the text in all but twelve seconds.

"Stop." were the only words she said and the only words that needed to be said. There was always an unconditional trust he held in her voice. No matter if it was honest, or even entirely contrary to his impulse, he couldn't help but hold faith in her intention. William dropped the gun. In an instant, Walters' fist rocketed into the boy's face, sending him flying backwards.

"Brat," Walter announced in his usual bone rattling bravado, but no response came from William; he just lay there on the ground, his eyes reflecting the clouds above.

"What about this one?" Jaden unearthed the knife, pointing it towards Ephriam, glaring as he focused and poised himself with one arm above his head, and the other extending from his waist like a fencer on quarte

"Both good, both founded this island, both not their fault, things turned out this way." Laila felt a rush to her head, she grabbed at the corner of her eyes and sat in the grass with her hands on her face. Jaden pushed the man away and strolled over to the girl.

"You know it's a bit more complex, there's a very intriguing chapter about regime politics that can be likened-" Ephriam bore the same unauthoritative countenance about his students and each who turned to him, and even the scholar himself could feel the interest of the audience dissipating. "You kids, what is wrong with you? This is why you need to stay in school! This!"

"So how old is Ephriam?" Jaden sided with Laila.

"Way older than you think," she said, shutting her eyes tight.

"Older than Walter?"

"I think so," she replied, regaining composure.

"Propaganda or not, this is bad! I mean, really bad! This is no peccant offense, there's a dead government official!" Ephriam prodded the man's chest with his foot. "Oh my! If the occident finds out his last location, they'll put a bounty on-" Ephram's voice cracked, he wretched up some spittle and held his chest as fear rattled his body.

"Older than the town?" Jaden leaned over. Laila deadpanned him and stood up; her left leg wobbled a little, but she managed to steady it, then walked over to William's side. Jaden, still pressing her with his inquiries.

"You see how dangerous the seas can be! It's not just what it can do to you, it's also what it can turn you into! Just learn to be a kid, play games with your friends, go on walks through the forest, dream up places you can never go, but forget all those ideas you have about manhood, and especially my boat! " Walter continued to rant at William, who simply lay on the ground. Feeling the grass brush the back of his neck, and the dirt cool his back.

Ephriam looked over, free from his pompous midst and saw as the sun reflected in William's eyes.

"Wait, how old is the town?" Jaden paused his questioning as Laila looked over at William, still lying on the ground.

"You will never get in my boat! Much less to sea so-" Walter cut himself off as he watched Laila hang over William. Her locks dangled over her ears and danced atop her head like the sun's beams. She gave him a look that relayed her conviction towards his passion, and grounded his motivation in something he could believe in himself. There were no words that they exchanged; instead, their intentions once more melted together, as their eyes conveyed all language they could speak. Instinctively, William smiled. Truly, a sight that would settle the heart of any man. Even the pragmatic chest of Walter and the judicious breast of Ephriam.

"Awwww," Ephriam let out.

"Sorry you got hit," she finally opened up, brushing hair from her forehead, and extending her hand, only to brush the same lock in the same direction. William got up and balanced himself with his back straight.

"It's okay," he said, rubbing his cheek, blank emotionless state having returned.

"I think I kind of deserved it." He got to his feet and stretched, then looked back at Laila, who looked away from him, and pursed her lips to the side as she began to reply.

"Yeahh…" her response dragged on.

"Just let me know if I'm close. Three-hundred-sixty-three?" Jaden used both fingers to display the numbers.

"What's he going on about?" William pointed.

"History textbook." Laila half-rolled her eyes until her indifference led her to fold her arms. "You know you can just read the book, it's literally right there." William pointed to the book, and Jaden shrank back in disgust.

"Ew, it has man's brains on it." They both shot Jaden a grimacing glare.

"Take the ship." Walter interrupted

"Thanks, Walter, man!" Jaden yelped excitedly.

"Take care," he said, hugging Laila, mussing her hair about, giving her head a playful nudge.

"You're just going to send them off to sea?" Ephriam fixed his collar with a heightened irritation.

"Oh come on, Ephy, you know as well as I, all the evils of this world comes to this island. It's no wonder the boys all hung up on blood and vengeance. Look in his eyes, you've seen how dark they've become. He needs to let a little more light in, more than we have on this island. Some time away will teach all of them more than you and I combined." Walter announced. "AND you!" Walter called over to William. "Make sure you keep her safer than you keep yourself." He hugged him and whispered into his ear. " Stick to your guns, not mine." The words may have well been spoken at arm's length, the gesture stirred no feelings in William, although the message had been received. Alicia had arrived much later than anyone present. She had followed Ephriam's lead, but his movements were much more brisk than her near-sighted eyes were capable of tracking. She had no idea of what had actually occurred, but looking at the scene that unfolded made her mind race with possibilities. She remained timid in the bushes for the danger to her hadn't seemed over until she felt her hand grasped, looking as Jaden absent-mindedly took flight after William, she turned towards Laila, who shot her what should have been a reassuring glance, if it wasn't stained with blood and sin.

"So it's over?" Alicia finally managed to get out.

"Yup." Laila led her out of the bushes, past the man, where flies had begun gathering.

"I can't believe you're rewarding this kind of behavior," Ephriam scratched his head as the duo passed by. They were now past Walter, who was stoically resigned as ever, beginning his trek towards the coast. Laila led Alicia past every detail that would now become etched into her mind as home. She never realized how much of her tiny home was unrecognized by her. It made her all the more regretful upon viewing the world-encompassing ocean as it appeared from the bay. The shoddily made wooden bridge juts out to a small wooden ship. The sight slammed into Alicia's head, and she made a short retreat back through the sand, still holding tight to Laila.

"We're leaving the island? Isn't this a little fast?" Alicia questioned, her eyes becoming dizzy with uncertainty. Laila's eyes softened and before any weariness overtook her, she began to turn around, still holding onto Alicia's hand who kept up with the pace. Alicia's heart began to race and move ahead of her footsteps, prompting her to question if it was her body or mind that was incapable of following the girl's lead.

"Look, I'm sorry, I'm just a little young to be setting sail. I don't even really know how, but that's probably because I haven't finished school, and-" They were now at the foothold of the wooden bridge. This is when Alicia separated herself from Laila.

"I see the future waiting for me on this island. I think I'd rather be anywhere else." Laila laughed briefly, then returned to looking into the distance.

"Then, how about we try this after we finish school? You're a fast learner, you know you'll be done in no time." Only a sea breeze answered Alicia, carrying with it a few locks of Laila's hair. She placed her hand over them, and watching this gesture was how Alicia realized.

"Go, I'll catch up, I promise." With those words, Laila embraced Alicia tightly, and the two shared in each other's warmth, before Laila darted off through the little window, to the life she always watched so vigilantly. Leaving Alicia, tears streaming down the sides of her cheek and dampening the sand around her, blurring her vision until she could see neither the horizon nor the waves, only Laila across the bridge and jumping onto the ship.

"Alright, it was your job to stock for the next voyage. I'll bring something extra if you can wait.

"Hey Walter, I know how to stock up for a voyage." William sighed.

"Okay, and when the storm comes-"

"Move into the waves, I know Walter- it wasn't me who put all those patches in the hull." William justified.

"That's right, you always bring the ship back as you left it."

"We may not see each other for a while, old man. Are you gonna finally admit I was your best employee?"

"You were my only employee, and I fired you," Walter laughed at the notion. Jaden spat with a *"plbttt"* from trying to hold in his laughter, and Laila covered her mouth as her eyes almost rolled to the back of her head.

William watched the joy grow in the moment. Laughter bounced from the planks, the salty winds muffled their voices, and they swayed with the sea as the mirth wormed its way into their limbs. It was at that moment that everyone on the ship realized how long it would be until they would laugh together like this again, and how many moments were wasted that they could have enjoyed in the same manner. He chuckled a little. William tried not to let his realization spoil the moment, but he wasn't alone. Even Walter had begun to feel as if he stayed any longer, it would delay their departure. He checked the sails one last time.

"You all know where you're headed?" Walter tightened the knot on the mast.

"No, but we won't be at sea long; we found a map Sandra made." Laila unfolded the paper.

"The shapes are definitely outlined better, and this middle part is a lot bigger, but yeah, this is way better than what the Occident is trying to push." Walter hovered over Laila's head, eyeing the map.

"What do you mean push? They probably just guessed wrong." Jaden questioned.

"Alright, I'm gonna go grab that food. You all try not to get too impatient now, you hear?"

"Hey Walter, thanks for everything," William said, and Walter's eyes began to well with pride.

"It's freshly caught, and I just prepared it." Walter wiped at his face as he crossed the rickety bridge.

Walter hadn't taken long to grab and pack the rations, but once he had come to deliver the materials, he saw the ship sailing out over the horizon.

"Be safe!" Ephriam yelled out, and the reality of the departure finally impacted Walter.

"Practice Math! Keep reading books! Drat, you might have to learn new languages to read! *Au revoir*!" Ephriam blubbered, watching as the ship went sailing into the distance. Alicia practically ran to the end of the shoddily made bridge, continuing to wave away at the trio. "Now that that's over, I could really use a drink." Ephriam stretched his arm and tried to grab one of the wrapped smoked fish, but Walter slapped his hand.

"What about you?" Ephriam sniffled and attempted to hand Walter a mostly used handkerchief. Walter stared at the cloth for a while before answering.

"I can't drink."

"You can't be that bad of a drunk,"

"Bye! Shit, I mean!" Alicia's movements were slowing, but the tears came down more rapidly than ever, although she was no more visible to them than they were to her. It had taken a while for her to accept the sight before her. It sunk in, sure enough, she dragged her feet across the wooden board, placing her feet so far up, the toes of her shoes hung off the dock, the same wind blew through her hair, and the sails.

"Until then!" she wiped her tears, smiling with an irremovable satisfaction. She lifted her fingers up to where her glasses used to sit and attempted to fix them, but before she got too close to her face, she realized how much had come from seeing the world with a new lens. The lens she would have never seen if the glasses hadn't broken, and she hadn't been able to see herself. A person in wholeness, regardless of which aspect others perceive. She moved her hand up to her chest, then raised it to the night sky, regaining her youthful vitality. She felt an overwhelming sense of energy build in her and went running off to her own adventure.

DO NOT READ THIS PAGE FIRST. THIS IS NOT A SUMMARY. IT'S A SEND OFF!

The Zodiac Proposition Sets Sail!

It's finally here everyone! The Zodiac Proposition is now a published series. I'm so excited to go on this journey with you all, but this has been a project at least twelve years in the making so I want to give credit where credit is due. To my family, uncles, aunts, cousins, nieces, nephews, brothers, sisters, and my mother; thank you for supporting me with this, and supporting me while I completed this project. To my friends and tribe, thank you for keeping my capacity up, and freeing up space for me to have such wild and absurd ideas. Thank you to those who helped me develop some of that absurdity, and emboldened me to share it with the world. The ones who helped me beta read and edit, helped with promotional and cover material, or just showed excitement for my passion. Thank you to all who inspired this project, including creatives and artists that have touched my heart who I've never had the opportunity to actually meet in-person but have fueled my craft nonetheless. I want to thank the entire publishing team at Franklin Publishing. You truly helped elevate my manuscript and write even truer to my original vision. Luca, Sophie, and Robby; The Zodiac Proposition would not be what it is without your input and feedback. We would still be shared from a web drive if it wasn't for your expertise and faith in this series. Lastly I want to give a shoutout to my partner, girlfriend, and love Danielle for the support, comfort, inspiration, motivation, belief, and for her otherworldly loyalty to a self-employed artist publishing their first novel. I am excited to bring you all this series and I truly hope that if this doesn't directly change the world for the better, I hope it inspires you and other readers to at least make the effort. We got a journey coming up, and I'm proud to say I'll be bringing you all more stories from this series for years to come. Welcome to The TZP Verse!

Acknowledgements

Patricia King

Danielle Martin

Ryan Perry

Troy Ramadin

Tafari John-King

Quentin Holt

Carlos Walton

R. John Quisenberry

Sophie Brown

Robby Reyes

Luca Romero

www.ingramcontent.com/pod-product-compliance
Lightning Source LLC
Chambersburg PA
CBHW060418310726
48976CB00003B/1107